sto

FRIENDS
OF ACPL

Y0-EHU-670

ALMOST COUSINS

ALSO BY ELIZABETH HARROVER JOHNSON

The Mysterious Trunk

ALMOST COUSINS

BY

ELIZABETH
HARROVER
JOHNSON

Illustrated by Bernard Case

IVES WASHBURN, INC.   NEW YORK

COPYRIGHT © 1961 BY ELIZABETH HARROVER JOHNSON

All rights reserved, including the right to reproduce this book, or parts thereof, in any form, except for the inclusion of brief quotations in a review.

Library of Congress Catalogue Card Number: 61-12756

MANUFACTURED IN THE UNITED STATES OF AMERICA

DEDICATED TO

1156234

DAVID

AND KITSY, GAIL, BEAVER, ANNE, NANCY, KATHERINE, JONATHA, WENDY, BETH, AND LISA, BECAUSE THEY ARE ALMOST COUSINS AND ALWAYS FRIENDS.

ALMOST COUSINS

1.

THE FRONT DOOR of a house in a Chicago suburb slammed shut. "Mother!" John Stevens shouted. "I got my report card."

"Here I am," came the answer from the kitchen.

"Just look at this," he said and proudly handed the report to his mother.

She sighed and read in a flat voice, "Promoted to Ninth Grade."

"Look at that science grade." John was so enthusiastic over the report card that he failed to notice his mother's worried look.

"That's fine," she said, giving John a pat on the shoulder.

"Fine! It's more than fine. That's the best report card I ever got. And look at that A in science. They don't just hand those things out for free, you know. Now don't you agree that I deserve to go to Cape Cod?"

[3]

"Yes, dear," his mother replied. "I'm very proud of your grades. Really I am. We'll talk about Cape Cod later." She left the kitchen hurriedly.

"How do you like that?" John threw his report card on the table. "I study until I almost collapse and all she says is 'fine.'" He was disappointed and confused by his mother's indifference so he opened the refrigerator and looked for something to eat. Nothing seemed appetizing. All he could find was a dish of canned peaches, one piece of salami, and another of hard cheese. He looked for something interesting to drink. The pantry had only cartons of empty soda bottles, so he settled for four slices of bread. Then he grabbed his tennis racket and slammed out the kitchen door. He walked into the warm June afternoon munching the bread and searching for a friend who could think of an interesting way to celebrate the end of the school year.

By the time John got home for dinner he had forgotten his mother's unusual mood of the afternoon. He had played Stevie Hemphill three sets of tennis. In the first two sets Stevie had taken him 6 to 2, 6 to 4. Then John had settled down to his game and walloped Stevie in the third set, 6 to 0.

"Dad home yet?" he called.

"We're in the living room," his father answered.

"Did you see my report card?"

[4]

"John," his father said in a very serious voice, "come in and sit down."

What in the world have I done now? John thought frantically. His parents were sitting on the sofa and his mother still looked unhappy.

"We've had word today that Grandad Ross has had a heart attack," his father announced.

"Oh!" John was shocked at the news yet at the same time comforted by it. So that's why his mother hadn't seemed to care about his report card. She was worried about Grandad. He sat down beside his mother and touched her hand. "Is he very sick?" he asked.

His mother nodded.

"Your mother must go to Indiana to take care of him," his father explained, "until he's well enough to live alone again, or come to Chicago to live with us."

"I hope he comes to live with us," John said. "Then he and I can go to the museum every week-end instead of just when he is here for a visit."

"As you came in," his father said, "we were discussing your plans for the summer."

"My plans!" John seemed surprised. "But Dad, my plans are already settled. Remember? This month I'm going to mow all the lawns I've agreed to mow and start a savings account for my microscope. And then in July Mother and I are going to Cape Cod." John settled back on the sofa as if the matter were dismissed.

[7]

"John," his mother said quietly, "I can't leave you here alone while I go take care of Father."

"Mother, I'm not a baby! I'm almost fourteen years old and I'm going into high school this fall. I can certainly get my own lunch and Dad will be home at night."

"I won't be home every night," his father explained. "I have scheduled several trips to branch offices and I shouldn't postpone them." John's father had recently been promoted to sales manager of a large manufacturing company.

"I could stay with Stevie Hemphill," John suggested. "Remember, he stayed with us once when his parents went away."

"That would be fine if we knew how long this illness would be," his father answered. "But it could be all summer. That is too long for you to visit Stevie. And it's definitely too long for you to stay alone here in the daytime."

John stared at his father.

"I think it would be best if you'd come to Indiana with me," his mother said. "I feel sure you could find lawns to mow there and you could still save your money for the microscope."

John continued to stare at his father.

"Now if you don't want to go to Indiana," his father went on, "it isn't too late to go to camp. I think we can find one that still has a vacancy."

John hadn't heard a word about going to Indiana. He

[8]

hadn't heard a word about going to camp. "*All summer,*" he repeated his father's words in a daze. "Do you mean that I can't go to Cape Cod? Do you mean that I can't enroll at the museum?"

2.

JOHN STAYED in the living room arguing with his father while his mother went to the kitchen to prepare dinner. He didn't mean to argue. He meant to stress only four important points: he *didn't* want to go to camp and he *didn't* want to go with his mother to Indiana; he *did* want to stay home and mow lawns and save the money for a microscope; he *did* want to go to Cape Cod. His arguments were all based on one thing: he was planning to be a scientist.

John's interest in science was not a recent development. He had decided in the first grade that he was going to be a scientist and he hadn't changed his mind since. He hadn't been exactly sure what kind of scientist he'd be, but as his father had once reminded him when he was eight years old, "You have plenty of time yet in which to specialize."

When his second-grade class had a unit of study on

seeds, he had been particularly commended by the teacher. In the fourth grade the unit of study was on the solar system and again he had been praised for his exceptional grasp of the subject. It was little wonder that he grasped the subject. He was a steady visitor to the museums.

The year he was in the sixth grade his parents had given him a microscope for Christmas. By the time he was in the seventh grade John had decided he had outgrown this "childish" microscope. His father had agreed that a "grown-up" microscope like those used in colleges would be a fine thing. "But," he had said, "it's a large order for old Santa Claus. This time you earn the money to buy it."

Because of John's constant scientific talk and trips to museums, his parents were not surprised when he had decided last summer that the highest point of interest on Cape Cod was its Junior Museum of Natural History. They discovered the museum quite accidentally one day when they were driving down the highway. John suddenly shouted, "Stop, Dad! A museum!"

His father jammed on the brakes and said in a teasing voice, "I thought you were on a vacation."

By the time the Stevens family came out of the museum an hour later, John had decided on his science specialty. It was Cape Cod. He had already begun to memorize the Cape shell life, its native birds, and the fish which abounded in the offshore waters. He had studied the displays which explained the glacial history of the Cape and the rock formations deposited by the receding glacier. And after that he had studied a small booklet which he found on an information table.

"The Cape Cod Junior Museum of Natural History," he read, "is an institution that was conceived and built up on the basis of a direct connection with its natural environment. Its purpose is to help children in the study of nature . . ." He scanned the words hurriedly, then read carefully, "Classes have been held in various branches of natural history every spring, summer, and fall for children between nine and fourteen."

Somewhere on the long drive home from the Cape to Chicago John had exacted a promise from his parents that they would arrange for him to study at the museum next summer. The months flew by. Next summer had become this summer. John and his mother were due to leave for the Cape in two weeks. But now his grandfather was ill and John tried to convince his father that he could not possibly go to Indiana or to camp. He did not attempt to disguise his disappointment over not going to the Cape as promised.

His father listened patiently for a while, then said slowly but firmly, "I am sympathetic with the fact that you had counted on earning money for a microscope, and that this is the last summer you can study at the museum. And I realize that when you plan to do a thing you are not easily dissuaded. But I am more concerned that your grandfather is ill. If he gets well quickly you will still be able to go to the Cape. Only time will tell about that. But John, further argument is useless. I want you to accept this change in plans and try to comfort your mother when she is so worried about her father."

John looked at his hands. He interlocked his fingers and twisted his thumbs around each other. His jaw was tight and the muscles of his throat ached from swallowing the tears. He had never faced such a bitter disappointment.

"Dinner's ready," his mother called.

"With all of this talk," his father said as they walked to the dining room, "I haven't had a chance to tell you how proud I am to have a son who brings home such an excellent report."

These words were more than John could bear. He swallowed hard and snuffed loudly.

"There are so many things to do before leaving that I hardly know where to begin," John's mother said at the dinner table.

"Just tell us what to do," his father said, "and John and I will help you. Won't we, John?"

John nodded bravely.

"For one thing," she continued, "I'll have to write to Laura and tell her that we won't be visiting her after all."

"How long has it been since you last saw her?" John asked.

"The day we graduated from college. That was seventeen years ago."

"Ann, why don't you call her instead of writing," John's father suggested. "At least you could have a telephone visit."

Mrs. Stevens' college friend, Laura Brown Reese, lived with her husband and child in a college town in New Jersey. The two had remained very good friends throughout the years, though their correspondence had dwindled to long notes on Christmas cards. The Stevenses had planned to take a side trip and visit the Reeses when they drove east to Cape Cod.

When dinner was over, John and his father washed dishes while his mother called Mrs. Reese in New Jersey. The conversation was so long that John was puzzled by what his mother was saying.

"Laura, that's so very nice of you. Yes, we'll talk it over with John and I'll call you back.

"John, Laura has invited you to visit them for the summer," Mrs. Stevens said when she had hung up. "She is sure you can find lawns to mow in College Park. Furthermore, they are near the ocean and spend most of their week-ends on the Jersey shore. And she says to be sure to bring your tennis racket. Brownie loves to play tennis."

[14]

"How many children do they have?" John wanted to know.

"Just the one child, Brownie."

"How would I get there?"

"You would take the train to New York. The Reeses would meet your train and drive you to College Park."

"Train to New York," John repeated, a hint of interest in his voice. "Well," he said with some hesitation, "the part about lawns to mow sounds good. And the ocean. And the tennis."

"Then it's settled," his father said enthusiastically. "We'll call Laura back right away and arrange the train schedule."

"This does make me feel better," Mrs. Stevens said after talking again to Mrs. Reese. "John, I just know you'll have a good summer after all."

John managed a grin. He was making a genuine effort to bury his disappointment over Cape Cod. "By the way," he said to his mother, "how old is he?"

"He?" Mrs. Stevens looked puzzled. "Whom do you mean?"

"Brownie Reese. The boy I'm going to visit."

There was a long pause before his mother answered. "John, I thought you knew. Brownie is a girl. She was named for her mother, Laura Brown Reese."

[15]

3.

THE NEWS THAT Brownie Reese was a girl sent John plunging up the stairs to his room. He threw himself face down on his bed. It was bad enough to have to abandon the trip to Cape Cod. But this! He felt such grim, black despair that he didn't hear his father's first knock on the door. At the second knock, he managed to raise up on his elbow and say weakly, "Come in."

His father took one look at him and asked, "Have you already forgotten that your grandfather is ill?"

"I'm sick too," John answered bitterly.

"What is the matter with you?"

"I don't want to spend a whole summer with a dumb girl I don't even know. Why didn't Mother warn me she was a girl before I agreed to go?"

A long, long conversation followed. Mr. Stevens tried to convince John that girls were as nice as boys. He

pointed out that since John was an only child he hadn't gotten to know many girls.

"This will be a grand opportunity for you to find out how nice a sister can be," which turned out to be the worst statement he could possibly have made.

"How nice a sister can be!" John said with a scowl. "You should hear what some of the boys say about their sisters."

"What, for instance?"

"That they are nothing but pests and that I'm lucky not to have one cluttering up the house."

The discussion on girls ended exactly where the one

on going to Indiana had ended earlier. Mr. Stevens told John in no uncertain terms to accept the situation gracefully and not to worry his mother with his unhappiness.

Breakfast the next morning was a peaceful affair. John seemed to have resigned himself to the situation.

"First thing I've got to do is see Stevie Hemphill and find out if he'll mow the lawns I promised to cut," John said. "He wants a new English bike, so maybe he'll be glad to do them."

"You had better get the lawn business straightened out right away," his mother said, "because you need a fourth polio shot and I'll have to call and see if the doctor or his nurse can take care of you today."

"How about a booster shot for tetanus while you're there?" Mr. Stevens said, "Then the Reeses won't have to worry if you get a cut."

"Gee whiz, Dad, what are you trying to do? Ruin my tennis arm? Next thing you'll have me taking shots for hydrophobia because the dogs in New Jersey might be rabid."

"We won't go that far." His father laughed. "Even the *shots* for hydrophobia are serious."

When John left the breakfast table, he went in search of Stevie. His friend was sympathetic to the sad turn of events in John's life and agreed to mow three of the lawns.

"I can't do all six and have time to play in the tennis

tournament," he said. "Why don't you ask Charlie to do the other three? I'll go with you."

As they walked down the street, Stevie asked, "Are you going to be able to play tennis in College Park?"

"No."

"Don't they have any courts?"

"They have tennis courts all right," John said, "but I'm not going to play tennis with a dumb old girl."

"Who said you had to play with a dumb old girl?"

"Well, I'm staying with this family called Reese. And they have one child, and she's a girl just my age, and she likes to play tennis, and I bet I won't be allowed out of the house unless I play tennis with her."

"Boy, you're sure getting the bad breaks this summer," Stevie said. "Why did your parents pick out a family with nothing but a girl in it?"

"Old friend of my mother," John explained. "Met in college, and known each other for a thousand years. You know how it is. Big deal."

"So long as your families are such good friends," Stevie reasoned, "maybe you can treat her like one of the family and ignore her."

"Hmm," John said hopefully, "maybe I can."

Charlie was as sympathetic to the recent development in John's life as Stevie had been.

"What is there to do in New Jersey?" he wanted to know after he had heard the story.

[19]

"Tennis and the Atlantic Ocean is all I know," John said.

"What are you going there for if that's all there is?"

"I'm staying with friends of the family so Mother can take care of my grandfather. What I mean is, well, you see, they've been friends so long that they're really sort of like cousins."

"Any cousins to play with?" Charlie asked.

"Yeah, one girl."

"This isn't your summer, is it?"

"You know I've been thinking," Stevie said. "It might not be so bad after all. I've got some girl cousins and they're sorta fun sometimes."

"I've got some, too," Charlie said, "but they're mostly a nuisance. My parents make me be nice when I visit. 'You can choose your friends, but you have to make the best of your relatives,' they're always saying. Anyway," he added as sort of an afterthought, "sometimes they're kinda fun."

"Well, I've got to go pack my suitcase," John said. "Can you do the three lawns that Stevie can't?"

"Gosh, I'm sorry, John. I'd like to help you out but we're leaving in a couple of days to visit my cousins in Oklahoma. They're the cousins with horses to ride. Try Pete. I think he's going to be around all summer."

Pete welcomed the opportunity to mow three lawns.

"I've got nothing else to do all summer," he said, "so I might as well get rich."

"That takes a load off my mind," John said. "After all the talking I did to get the jobs, I'd hate to welsh out on the deal."

"Anything interesting to do in New Jersey?" Pete asked.

"It's hard to tell," John answered. "I'm visiting my cousin and she's a girl. And you know how it is. Sometimes they're fun and sometimes they're not."

4.

THE EXCITEMENT of taking the train to New York helped John temporarily to forget Cape Cod, microscopes, and girls. His parents and Stevie Hemphill came to see him off. Stevie told him over and over again what a big deal it was to be allowed to travel alone. His father explained about ordering meals in the dining car and tipping porters. His mother reminded him three times that he was to go straight from the train to the information booth in Grand Central Station where the Reeses would be waiting for him.

"Going to the information booth is easy," he said, "but how will they know me?"

"I told Laura to look for a tall thirteen-year-old with blue eyes and blond hair who would be carrying a big suitcase and a tennis racket," she answered. "Right?" John grinned.

[22]

Stevie's farewell statement to John was, "Good luck on your cousin and write to me."

The train ride to New York was fine but for one thing. It gave John time to remember. He thought of all the things he had seen in the Cape Cod museum, and all the things he had hoped to see in the microscope he had made such careful plans to buy. Fortunately something else occurred to him in time to save him from a sniveling case of self-pity over the summer ahead. He remembered that his grandfather was ill.

The walk from the station platform to the information booth in Grand Central Station was a long one. John's suitcase seemed to gain a pound with each step he took. His father had given him money for a porter, but John was afraid that he would never find his suitcase again if he let it out of his sight in New York City. So he carried it.

When he came into the concourse of the station, he started to look around for the information booth. But the immensity of the room and all the activity overwhelmed him. He set his suitcase on the floor and stood gawking like a tourist at the high ceiling and the blown-up Kodachrome on the wall until he was interrupted by someone saying,

"You must be John Stevens. We're the Reeses."

Three people were smiling at John—a man, a woman, and a brown-eyed girl with a blond ponytail.

[23]

"You're the only boy who came through the train gates with a tennis racket," Brownie said pleasantly.

Greetings over, the trip from New York City to College Park was hard on John. The Reeses insisted on being friendly and were anxious to entertain him when all he wanted was to be allowed to sit quietly in a corner of the car. First off, they wanted to know if his trip had been a good one. Then they asked if he was hungry. When he assured them that he wasn't tired and he wasn't hungry, they drove along the Hudson River and crossed over the George Washington Bridge because it was a clear day and they wanted him to see the New York skyline. All during the drive he had to sit by Brownie and be as nice to her as she was to him. Yes, he could see the Empire State Building. No, he'd never heard of the Palisades. Yes, it was nice of her to have borrowed a bike for him from a friend who was going away to camp. Yes. No. Yes. No.

It wasn't that John really and truly disliked girls. He was nice enough to them at school. Of course they slowed down the science class, but he knew they couldn't help it if they weren't great scientists. But when the school bell rang at three o'clock in the afternoon, he could go off with his friends and forget about girls until nine o'clock the next morning. He realized as he sat in the back seat of the car on the drive to College Park that being nice to Brownie was going to be different. It was no nine-to-three job. It was going to be a twenty-four-hour proposition.

As soon as John had been shown the guestroom, Brownie began to make all kinds of suggestions about something interesting for him to do. They could play a game of tennis. John didn't think so. She could get two friends and they'd play doubles. John didn't think so. She'd show him the town and let him meet her friends. John didn't think so.

At this point Mrs. Reese said, "You have plenty of time to do those things, Brownie. Maybe John would like to rest in his room before dinner."

"Yes, I would," he answered gratefully.

In a few moments there was a knock on his door and Brownie's voice called, "John."

John opened the door thinking, "A guy can't have two minutes of peace around here." The expression on his face showed his annoyance.

"Here is the weekly paper," Brownie said. "There are several ads for someone to mow lawns."

"Thanks," John said. He took the paper and politely closed the door in her face.

Brownie hurried down the stairs and into the kitchen. "Mother," she said, "what have I done to him? He doesn't like me."

"Brownie!" Her mother looked up from the mixing bowl with a look of disbelief. "What could possibly make you think such a thing? I was just thinking that I had never met such a polite boy."

"That's what I mean. He's too polite. All he says is 'yes' and 'no' and 'thanks.'"

"You must remember that John has had very upsetting news about his grandfather."

"That's no reason for him to dislike me."

"Now, now," her mother said, "give the boy time to get acquainted. I'm sure he doesn't dislike you."

"I'm not so sure," Brownie was about to say, when she looked up and saw John standing in the kitchen doorway with the newspaper in his hand.

"Hey, Brownie," he said in an enthusiastic voice.

Brownie's mother smiled and turned back to the mixing bowl.

"Is this ad a joke or is it for real?" He read aloud from the paper Brownie had so recently delivered to his room and about which he had seemed so annoyed. "Bats Wanted for Science. Desire Information Leading to Their Location. Ho 2-6300, Ext. 135."

In contrast to the ride from Grand Central Station to College Park, Brownie found that the dinner hour with John was most pleasant. They talked about bats. John and Brownie decided that the ad for bats was the work of a prankster. Mr. Reese reminded them that Ho 2-6300

[26]

was the University telephone number and that some of the scientists might very well need bats for research.

"Do you know anything about bats?" Brownie asked John. The only thing she knew about bats was that although they flew, they were not birds, but mammals which gave birth to live babies. Also, she knew that she didn't care for them. By the time dessert was served Brownie had concluded that John knew quite a bit about bats. What was even more surprising, her father knew something about them, too.

John knew some of the species of bats. He had named the big brown bat, little brown bat, fruit bat, horseshoe bat, and long-eared bat, when Brownie interrupted with,

"Don't forget the vampire bat. I've heard they suck your blood until you fall down and simply die of weakness."

"You're at the dinner table, Brownie," her father reminded her.

John told them that a baby bat was born naked and pink and clung to its mother's breast while she darted in flight. And when the mother came to rest she folded her wings around it to keep it warm. He knew that a bat had a very efficient sonar system and that scientists had been making intensive studies of this system.

"You make them sound positively decent," Brownie said.

"Why don't you answer the ad tomorrow and see what

[27]

they want the bats for?" Mr. Reese asked. "You seem to know so much about them that it might be interesting. And it might get you in the laboratory."

"Well, for one thing I don't know where there are any bats," John answered. "And I better see if I can locate some lawns to mow, or I'll never get that microscope."

So the subject of bats was dropped—for the time being.

5.

JOHN WAS UP bright and early the next morning. He had underlined those ads in the paper which had to do with lawn mowing. He propped the paper by the telephone and began to dial. Two people were anxious that he come around to see them right away, because they were trying to leave on vacation and wanted to be sure their lawns would be taken care of in their absence.

"Brownie, where's a pencil?" he yelled. "I've got to write down these addresses."

Brownie came on the run like an obedient slave anxious to please its master. She even offered to guide him to the addresses. Once more a look of annoyance swept his face. He started to say no, he'd find his way alone, but then thought better of it. He couldn't ignore his cousin yet; he'd been here only twenty-four hours.

He soon regretted his kindly and thoughtful decision.

Brownie seemed to know everyone they met on the quiet, tree-lined streets of the town, and she insisted on introducing him as her friend from Chicago who was visiting for the summer. At each introduction he was just about to explain they were really more like cousins than friends. But somehow he couldn't get up the nerve to correct her.

"Hey, Brownie. Missed you playing tennis yesterday!"

"Hi, Tom. I went to New York to meet my friend." Brownie introduced John to Tom Jackson.

"I lost the doubles match without you," Tom said. "Had to grab myself another partner and she wasn't nearly as good a player as you."

John experienced great success in his job hunting. He went to see two people and he found two lawns to mow. One of the jobs included a lot of weeding of fancy flower beds. The owner had wanted to know whether he was a good weeder and he had assured her he was. However, the truth of the matter was that he specialized only in mowing lawns with a power mower and was not a fancy trimmer or weeder. It seemed to him that was a woman's job. At least his mother did it at home. But he figured out that if he didn't weed and trim, he wouldn't get the jobs. Without the jobs, he wouldn't get the microscope, so the weeding didn't seem as heavy a task as it had seemed at home.

Because he claimed to be a good weeder, the woman recommended him to a friend who lived on the edge of

town. Brownie guided him there, and it wasn't long before he had three lawns to mow. He was feeling quite set up and pleased with the world after this successful job-hunting expedition. He stopped mumbling answers to Brownie on the way home and talked to her. Brownie proved to be such a good listener that he forgot she was a girl and told her how much the microscope would cost.

He was on the point of telling her about the lens power of the microscope when they met a bunch of chattering girls. It was John's poor luck that Brownie knew them and introduced him as her friend. The girls giggled and looked at each other and said, "Hi, John," and he wished he was at the bottom of Cape Cod Bay. John did not talk to Brownie during the rest of the walk home. He disappeared into his room the moment they returned.

"Mother, I simply don't understand him," Brownie said. "Sometimes he's nice and sometimes he's simply awful."

"I presume you're referring to John?" her mother asked.

"Yes."

"Perhaps we don't understand the boy," her mother admitted. She stopped making sandwiches for lunch and sat down at the kitchen table. "Something may be worrying him besides his grandfather's illness. When is he nice and when is he awful, as you say?"

"Well . . ." Brownie started and then thought awhile.

[33]

"He was awful coming home from New York yesterday. Then he was nice last night at dinner. He was awful this morning when we went to see about the lawns. He wasn't at all nice to my friends. Then he got nice when he was telling me about the microscope he was going to buy."

Mrs. Reese listened patiently as Brownie recalled the first puzzling twenty-four hours of John's visit.

"Then we met some of the girls on the way home and they were as friendly as they could be but he started being all creepy and hating me again, and you can see it doesn't make a bit of sense."

"I'm not so sure about that," her mother said. "He was nice last night at dinner and you'll recall that was when he was talking about bats and what use scientists might have for them. Today you say he was friendly when he was talking about his microscope."

"Now I get it," Brownie interrupted before her mother could finish drawing her conclusions. "He's only nice if he's talking about science." She picked up the kitchen phone and started dialing.

"Hello. Is this the University? I'd like Extension 135, please. Hello," she said again, "is this the party who advertised for bats? Oh, it is. Do you really want bats? For science?"

Brownie listened intently. "Thank you very much," she said and hung up. From the front hall, she called upstairs, "Hey, John!"

The door of John's room opened and he answered with a loud, grumbling, "Yes?"

"That ad's no joke," Brownie said, her voice full of excitement. "There's a man at the University who really wants bats. He's on some important research project and he can't take time out to search for all the bats he needs."

As Brownie talked, John gradually made his way down the stairs.

"He said that if you find any bats, tell him where they are and he'll go catch them."

Suddenly John became a different boy from the one who had returned from the job hunt. He began to tell Brownie about an article he had read that told of experiments with bats proving they didn't use their eyes to catch insects for eating. They used their echoes instead.

"Oh, no!" Brownie said. She was so impressed and listened so intently that John told her in even greater detail about the article.

"But," he concluded, "I don't know where to find any bats." 1156234

"Don't worry, I'll find you some bats," Brownie said confidently and returned to the kitchen. She whispered to her mother. "We're talking about bats and he's suddenly nice again." Then she added with grim determination, "Since that's what it takes to make him happy, I'm going to find him some of those nasty, creepy things if it's the last thing I ever do."

[35]

6.

BROWNIE INVITED John to play a set of tennis that afternoon. Although he was eager to play he declined the invitation politely and said that he had to start mowing lawns right away. He knew there was really no need for him to be in such a hurry about the lawns because there wasn't that much work involved. The truth was that he could not quite bring himself to play a game of tennis with a girl.

That night Brownie was late for dinner. "She won't stop playing tennis as long as there's anyone to play with and light enough to see the ball," her father said. "We might as well eat."

Mr. and Mrs. Reese and John had no sooner sat down at the dinner table than Brownie came slamming in the front door.

"Hey, John," she called excitedly. "I've found some bats for you."

[36]

"Come on in to dinner and tell us about them," her mother answered from the dining room.

As Brownie's story of her afternoon unfolded, it developed that she had not been playing tennis as much as taking a census on bats.

"I asked all the people I met on Main Street if they had ever seen any bats around town," she said. "At first they wanted to know what the joke was. Then when I told them it was no joke because it was in the paper, they said they hadn't seen any bats. Finally, I met Mr. Jones. He's the postman," she explained to John. "He said that the Williams' house over on Grover Lane had bats in the attic."

"Right here in town?" John asked hopefully.

Brownie nodded and continued her story. "So I said thank you very much, I'll go right over and see them, and he said no need to bother, the Williamses were in Europe for the summer and the place was locked up and I best not go trespassing on their property."

"Aw shucks," John said.

"But that's not the end of the story," Brownie assured him.

"Brownie," her mother said, "please eat your dinner before it gets cold. Then you can finish your story."

John was puzzled as he ate dinner. Why had Brownie gone to so much trouble to find bats when she really liked to play tennis? Was she finding bats for him to take to the scientist? She had certainly said, "I've found some bats for you," when she came in to dinner. He didn't understand her.

"So," Brownie continued after she had swallowed the last bit of dinner whole, "I went on to play tennis. And I explained to Tom Jackson that I was late for the match because I had been looking for bats. And he said he knew there were plenty of them at the Hendricks' farm on Reeder Road. He's ridden by there at dusk and seen them swooping around the barn."

"I know where it is," Mrs. Reese said. "I used to buy my eggs from Mr. Hendricks."

"He's a wonderful old fellow," Mr. Reese said. "Has a big responsibility these days. His daughter's husband died and she and the children have moved in with him."

"How far away is the Hendricks farm?" John asked.

"About a mile," Brownie said. "And if you'd really like some bats to take to that scientist I'll be glad to show you the way."

"Let's go," John agreed and off they went on their bikes for a bat hunt. It was the first time since he had come to the Reeses that John forgot that he was venturing forth in broad daylight in the company of a girl.

"We're almost there," Brownie said as she started up a long, gently rising slope.

The Hendricks farm stretched before them in full view. A white house, somewhat in need of paint, stood fairly

close to the road. There was a large unpainted barn behind the house with smaller outbuildings clustered
around it. A slender woman was taking down clothes
from a clothesline in the back yard and a strange kind of
ball game was in progress around one of the outbuildings.
Shouts of "high-over" could be heard. An old man was
sitting in a rocking chair on the back porch intently
watching the game.

"Run, Jack, you can catch her," he called excitedly,
leaning forward in the rocker. "Hurry, Mary, or you'll
be it."

When the excitement of the game had died down and
the old man had resumed his rocking, John said: "Hello."

"Well, bless my soul, where'd you come from?" he
asked. "I was so busy watching the game of high-over
that I didn't know a soul was around."

"We came on our bikes," John said.

The old man had a crinkly, kindly face with a gay
twinkle in his eyes and the children liked him immediately. Brownie came forward with her ponytail bouncing as usual and a friendly smile on her face. "I'm
Brownie Reese and you must be Mr. Hendricks," she
said, "and this is my fr—"

John hastened to interrupt her and finish the sentence
to his own liking. "I'm her cousin, John Stevens," he said,
"and we were wondering if you had any extra bats
around that we could use."

"Cousin!" Brownie almost gasped aloud. "Cousin!" She recovered her equilibrium in time to hear Mr. Hendricks laugh and say,

"My barn is full of extra bats and they're all yours for the catching." He accompanied this statement with a broad sweep of his arm.

By this time the ballplayers had seen Brownie and John and came hurrying to the back porch like three friendly puppies. "This is Brownie Reese and her cousin, John Stevens," Mr. Hendricks said, "and these are my grandchildren, Mary, Jimmy, and Jack Mason. And this is their mother," he said of the pretty woman with the tired smile who approached the back porch with a basket of laundry.

"These young folks are bat hunting," Mr. Hendricks explained to his grandchildren. "And they want to know if we have extra bats."

"Extra bats! Are they kidding?"

John hastened to explain why they were looking for bats. Jack, the younger Mason boy, interrupted John's story with, "There's one now. They're already starting to come out for their evening meal." He pointed to a bat already etching its erratic flight-pattern across the quiet, darkening blue of the evening sky.

"You'd better hurry up if you want to catch bats tonight," Jimmy said to John. "I'll show you where they are."

"They're my bats, too," Jack said. "Let me show him, too." He trotted along after Jimmy and John. Seven-year-old Jack was sure that his big brother who was twelve and his big sister who was thirteen were always anxious to lose him when there was something interesting afoot.

"Do you want to go after bats?" Mary asked Brownie.

From the way she turned up her freckled nose as she asked the question, Brownie knew that Mary and she had something in common. They disliked bats. But she had resolved to overcome her dislike if it would help her gain John's friendship. She was sure she was finally on the right track. After all, she rationalized, he must like me. Why else did he tell Mr. Hendricks he was my cousin?

"Sure, I want to help catch the bats," she said and started for the barn.

"The best way to catch bats is to stay right out here," Mr. Hendricks called after the girls.

Mary laughed. "You're always kidding, Grandpa. How could we possibly catch bats out here?" and she ran off without waiting for his answer.

"There they are." Jimmy pointed to a dark cluster on the underside of the topmost beam in the darkest corner of the barn. "Maybe you can reach them from the ladder."

John looked at the long ladder, which went way up to the roof of the barn. He wasn't used to climbing great heights. There were only small, newly-planted trees in the suburban area where he lived and of course there were no great big barns to climb in. He had been to the top of tall buildings in Chicago, but he had ridden in an elevator where he couldn't look down as he went up.

"Have you ever caught a bat up there?" he asked Jimmy.

"Never wanted to," was the brief answer. "Don't like the teeth."

John started climbing briskly up the ladder. There's really nothing to this, he kept saying to himself. Then he made his big mistake. He looked up at the hanging bats, and down at the barn floor. His stomach twisted into a hard knot. His head began to spin and his knees to quake. He clung onto the rungs of the ladder for dear life.

Brownie noticed the frantic clutch of his hands. "Want me to come up and help you?" she called.

"Yes," John managed to answer gratefully. He felt braver with someone else on the ladder, even a girl.

Unlike John, Brownie suffered no fear of heights as she climbed toward the roof of the barn. She went up as if she had been climbing ladders all her life, hand over hand, foot over foot. The reason for her exceptional bravery on the high ladder was simple. She had no fear of heights because she was climbing with her eyes tightly shut.

"It isn't such a long climb when we have a good hay crop," Jimmy called to them.

"But it hurts almost as much to fall on a bale of hay as

[42]

it does to fall on the barn floor," Jack said. "I've done it a million times."

Brownie wished he'd keep quiet.

"I don't think I can reach them," John said, putting his hand out gingerly.

Brownie opened her eyes and found herself at the top of the barn. She started to look down and quickly changed her mind. She looked up instead. "Oh, no," was all she could say at her close-up view of the clump of bats. A dark-brown, furry, squeaking mass clung to the beam. At first glance it seemed to be one panting, breathing object, but on closer observation Brownie could make out the vibrating ears and the blinking, beady little eyes of individual, chittering bats hanging upside down on the beam and on each other.

John clung to the ladder with one hand and reached for a bat with the other. "I can't quite reach them," he said to Brownie. And then the bats began to move and some crawled along the beam and launched themselves into flight around the barn. Others inched through the eaves out of sight.

"You'd better get one before they all fly away," Jimmy called.

"Watch out one doesn't get in your hair," Mary shouted.

"You'll have to cut all your hair off to get it out," Jack added.

John was so intent on his bat hunt that he forgot his

fear of heights. He didn't even hear the shouts below, but Brownie heard every word. John still clung to the ladder precariously with one hand and made a vast sweep toward the bats with the other. At that very moment Brownie gave an absolutely bloodcurdling shriek.

"A bat! It's in my hair! Help! It's in my hair!"

7.

THE BAT HUNT was a failure. By now all the bats were darting around outside the barn gorging themselves on the insects which swarmed in the evening sky. The friendship which Brownie had so recently felt was developing nicely between John and her was at a complete standstill. They stood at the foot of the ladder shouting unpleasantries at each other while Mary and Jimmy listened uncomfortably. Jack was thoroughly enjoying the excitement.

"I had a bat right in my hand and you scared it with your crazy shouting," John accused Brownie.

"Well, how would you like to have a bat in your hair?"

"It wasn't in your hair. You just thought it was."

"It wasn't in your hand either."

"It's lucky for you that I didn't fall and kill myself

when you yelled. Why'd you have to come up the ladder anyway?"

"Why'd I have to come up the ladder? Because you looked scared, that's why," Brownie flashed back. Her ponytail bobbed violently.

"Me scared? Ha. That's a good one. Since when have I been scared of a little old ladder? I could climb that ladder with one hand tied behind my back."

"I double-dare you," Jack said. Even the freckles on his turned-up nose seemed to dance with merriment.

Jimmy pushed Jack and told him to stop talking, while Mary searched wildly for something to say to ease the situation. "The bats will be up there again tomorrow night," she said. "You could tell the scientist about them and maybe he could catch them."

"And maybe he'll have long arms and can reach the bats from the ladder," Jimmy said.

"Maybe so," John said, "but he's probably too old to climb the ladder." He felt dreadfully disappointed. He had so wanted to tell the scientist that he had bats for him. He had imagined saying to this brilliant man with rumpled, longish hair and an absent-minded smile: "Here is a bat I found. No, it was quite easy to catch. Nothing to it. I can catch all the bats you need, Doctor." And out of the corner of his eye as he talked to the scientist, he could see a row of microscopes lined up in the laboratory.

"Let's play high-over," Jack suggested. Things were getting dull again and he longed for more excitement.

"Yes, let's," Jimmy said.

Jack grinned proudly because his big brother was so enthusiastic about his suggestion. Usually he vetoed whatever Jack wanted to do.

"I don't know how to play," Brownie said.

"I never even heard of the game," John said.

"We'll teach you," Jack assured them, and they all rushed outside. But alas, dusk had descended while they were in the barn. Brownie and John remembered their promise to be home before dark.

"We'd better hurry," John said, and he and Brownie jumped on their bikes and rode off, calling back promises to come again and play high-over. Their gay voices had become quiet by the time they reached the foot of the hill. Brownie and John rode back to College Park in deadly silence. Each was thinking of how the other one had acted on the ladder.

Next morning, the front doorbell rang while the family was at breakfast. Brownie went to the door. When she returned to the kitchen she handed John a letter from his mother marked *Special Delivery*. He tore open the envelope hurriedly, thinking, "Grandfather is worse; no, he's better and we're going to Cape Cod after all." He read the letter rapidly. Then he stuffed it back in the envelope, jammed the letter in his hip pocket, and continued eating his breakfast with lowered head.

"Bad news?" Mr. Reese asked.

"No," John answered and took another mouthful of scrambled eggs.

"How is your grandfather?" Mrs. Reese asked, when it finally became apparent that John was not going to furnish any information about his family.

"Better, thank you, but Mother must still stay with him." He excused himself from the table and went to the telephone in the hall.

"That boy certainly had counted on going to Cape Cod," Brownie's father said.

"I feel so sorry for him," her mother said. "He's had such a big disappointment for a child his age."

Sorry for him indeed, Brownie thought to herself. They should have heard the way he yelled at me last night. I ought to tell them about the horrible bat hunt. But what's the point? They'd never believe how he yelled at me. He's always so proper and polite when they're around.

Brownie had decided one thing since last night. If he didn't want to be nice to her, she'd ignore him. Simply and utterly and completely ignore him. She'd be proper and polite when she had to, and the rest of the time she'd pretend he simply didn't exist.

"Hey, Brownie. Guess what?" John came hurrying back into the kitchen from the telephone. "Dr. Thomas wants to go out and catch some bats. He wants me to show him the way out to the Hendricks farm this evening."

John was once more the pleasant and outgoing friend

he had been on the way to the farm the night before. Brownie forgot that she was going to ignore him. "Do you think he can reach the bats from the ladder?" she asked.

"I didn't tell him exactly where they were," John said, "but he told me that he always catches them with a net, so I figure he shouldn't have any trouble."

"I never thought of a net," Brownie said. "That's certainly better than with your bare hands."

"Dr. Thomas said that if I was going to help him catch bats I should bring leather gloves. He said a bat bite can be quite serious. Are there any around I could borrow?"

Brownie immediately offered him her mother's best pigskin driving gloves.

John thought the day would never pass. He worked at lawn mowing in the morning. After lunch he ambled down to the University tennis courts to see what was going on there. He hadn't even seen a match since leaving Chicago, much less played one. Brownie was playing with Tom Jackson and John had to admit she was pretty good. When she noticed John watching her, she blew her game completely and Tom took the set. Both Brownie and Tom offered to let John play but he said he had to write a letter to a friend. John went back to his room and wrote a letter to Stevie Hemphill.

Dear Stevie:
Here I am in College Park, New Jersey. The train ride was great, especially the part where I ate in the dining

car. You'd never guess what I'm going to do. I'm going to help a real scientist catch some bats for his lab. You said good luck on my cousin when I left. She isn't so bad considering, but she's even dumber in science than the girls in our class. Well, good luck on your lawn mowing. I've got three to do.

Your friend,

JOHN

Finally the dinner hour came and went. John took Mrs. Reese's gloves, which Brownie had so generously loaned him, and sat down on the front steps to wait for Dr. Thomas. Brownie joined him about the time a battered old station wagon slowed down, then stopped in front of the house.

"Who's that?" John said as a young man got out of the car and started up the sidewalk.

"Looks like one of the college students," Brownie said. "Some of them work around here during the summer."

"Are you John Stevens?" the man asked.

"Yes, I am."

"I'm Bill Thomas. Are you ready to go for the bats?"

"Dr. Thomas!" John gasped. "But I didn't think you'd look like that!"

"What am I supposed to look like? A comic-book scientist with a long, black beard and thick glasses?" Bill Thomas asked with a twinkle in his eyes.

"I didn't exactly expect you'd have a crew haircut as

short as mine," John admitted. Then he remembered his manners and introduced Brownie to the scientist. "Dr. Thomas, I'd like you to meet my cousin, Brownie Reese."

"If we're going to hunt bats together, I think you'd better call me Bill," Dr. Thomas said as he acknowledged the introduction. "Well, are you ready to go?" he asked John, adding, "Would your cousin like to come too?"

Before Brownie could accept the invitation, John answered for her: "She doesn't like bats. She's afraid they'll get in her hair."

Brownie was so blinded by the tears in her eyes that she couldn't even see the station wagon when it pulled away from the curb. She had never been so disappointed and so humiliated. When she had finally got control of herself, she snuffed, wiped her eyes on the short sleeves of her blouse, and turned to go back into the house. It was then she noticed her mother's leather gloves lying on the steps. John had gone off and forgotten them.

Her first thought was that it served him right. Let him get bitten by a bat. But her second thought was more charitable. She remembered how much he wanted to help Bill, and how disappointing the summer had been to him so far. She picked up the gloves and went to tell her parents that she was bicycling out to the Hendricks farm with the gloves and would be back before dark. "I'll just throw these old gloves at him," she said to herself, "and turn right around and come home."

[53]

8.

"THEY'RE PLAYING high-over again," John said excitedly as Bill Thomas drove the station wagon in the driveway of the Hendricks farm. "Gosh, they sure must dirty a lot of clothes," he said, more to himself than to Bill, as he noticed Mrs. Mason at the clothesline. "Mrs. Mason was taking clothes off the line last night."

Jimmy, Jack, and Mary saw John and came on the run. "Where's your cousin?" Mary asked John.

"She didn't come."

John changed the subject and introduced everyone to Bill, who had been busy unloading a net and a small cage lined with fine screen wire. "Dr. Thomas!" they said.

Bill and John laughed at their surprise. "That's about what I said," John admitted, "but he says to call him Bill. Can I help you?" John asked Bill.

"You can get my leather gloves from the front seat."

Moments later John said, "Where are my gloves?" He

searched in the front seat and in his pockets. Then he remembered exactly where he had left them. "They're on the Reeses' front steps," he moaned.

"Don't get near the bats then," Bill cautioned.

"He got near them last night," Jack said, "and he didn't have any gloves on."

"Don't you know that bats can carry hydrophobia?" Bill said to John.

"Hydrophobia!" they all exclaimed.

"You're kidding," added John.

"No, I'm not kidding one little bit. You won't ever see me handling bats without leather gloves."

"I thought dogs and foxes were the only animals that carried rabies," Jimmy said.

"Bats can carry it too," Bill told them. "Not every bat carries rabies, to be sure, any more than every fox or dog does. But handling as many bats as I do, chances are pretty good that if I'm not careful, I'll run up against a rabid one someday, he'll bite me, and that'll be that."

"I thought doctors had shots to give you for hydrophobia," Mary said.

"They do, but I don't want to have those either if I can help it. The reaction from the shots alone can be serious."

"That's what Dad said," John recalled, thinking of the day before he had left Chicago when he had to rush around taking shots for polio and tetanus.

[55]

Grandpa had been sitting in his rocker on the back porch watching the goings-on in the driveway. Then he left the porch and joined the group gathered around Bill. He stood quietly listening to the conversation, looking over the cage and the net. "So you're one of those doctor fellows they have at the University," he said after John had introduced him to Bill.

Bill smiled and admitted he was.

"Is that where they taught you to catch bats in a butterfly net?" he asked bluntly.

Bill laughed heartily. "No, sir," he answered, "they didn't teach me that. But it's the easiest way I could figure to do it."

"Easiest way, easiest way," Grandpa grumbled. "All you young folks think about these days is the easiest way to do a thing. There's no sporting blood left in the lot of you. He started back toward his rocking chair, mumbling as he walked, "What a lot of trouble and monkey business over catching a few of those little critters."

"What do you want a bunch of dumb old bats for anyway?" Jack asked with the bluntness of his grandfather.

"They're really not dumb," Bill answered. "Scientists are learning a lot from them."

"Like what?"

"They're learning more about sonar, for instance." Bill smiled good-naturedly.

"Sonar," Jimmy repeated. "But that's what they have on ships."

"You mean you take the sonar out of these little old bats and put it in the ships and it works?" Jack asked with his eyes bugging out.

"Not quite." Bill laughed. "We study the bats to see how their sonar works. In turn, we apply this knowledge to man-made sonar devices."

"I don't understand exactly what sonar is," Jimmy said.

"Do you want the answer in scientific terms?" Bill said.

"Sure."

"Sonar is a term formed from the contraction of sound navigation and ranging. By means of sonar equipment, sonic or supersonic pulses are transmitted. Then these are reflected from an object, and received back where they started from. By measuring the time it takes for the sound to go to and return from the object, it is possible to measure the distance to that object."

"I get it," Jimmy said. "That's neat."

"What's that got to do with bats?" Jack didn't understand the explanation, but he wasn't going to say so.

"Some bats rely on their own natural sonar system rather than their eyesight," he explained to Jack. "For instance, when one of the bats in your barn is up in the air trying to find a moth to eat, it keeps sending out high-frequency sounds. These are reflected back to the bat from the moth and enable him to keep measuring the distance from his prey. In other words, it locates the moth by listening for the echoes of its own sound waves. Now, let's see your bats."

[57]

Jimmy and Jack led the way to the barn. Mary tagged along to watch the excitement.

"Where are they?" Bill asked.

"Up there."

Bill looked up toward the eaves of the barn, then at the ladder, then back toward the bats clinging beneath the beam.

"You can reach over from the ladder," John said, eager to convince Bill that he'd found bats that were easy to catch.

"When we have a good hay crop, you can touch them," Jimmy said.

"That's what you said last night," John said. "How do you figure that?"

"When the crop is good, the bales are piled way up to the beam where the bats roost."

"We used to take a stick and touch them," Jack chimed in, "and the whole mess would wiggle and squeak and climb around. They looked as if they were walking on broken wings."

"It's a miracle we aren't dead of hydrophobia." Jimmy shivered.

"I wish you'd had a good hay crop," Bill said, still surveying the height of the ladder and the remote colony of bats.

"So does Mother," Jack said, "because then she could have bought a washing machine."

[58]

"I might as well have a try at it." Bill put on the gloves and picked up the net. "But my chances aren't very good."

"Why not?" John was puzzled and disappointed.

"There's no top on this net," Bill explained, "and by the time I climb all the way back down the ladder, any bats I've caught will probably have escaped."

"What do you usually do for a top?" Jimmy asked.

"I caught the bats I've used so far in a cave up in the northern part of the state. I just reached over my head with the net, caught the bats, and quickly flicked them in the cage."

"Why don't you go up to the cave again?"

"It's quite far and I was hoping that my advertisement in the paper would reveal a source of bats closer to the lab."

"Why don't you flip the net over the rim like I used to do when I caught butterflies?" Jimmy asked.

"It's worth a try," Bill agreed.

John was so intent on watching him climb the ladder that he didn't hear anyone enter the barn until a voice near him said, "John." He jumped as if one of the bats had bitten him, turned, and faced Brownie.

"She had to follow me," he thought angrily. "She just had to poke into what I was doing even though she's scared to death of bats."

"You left your gloves on the steps," Brownie said, "so I brought them out to you. I thought you'd want to help

[59]

Bill catch a bat." But she had seen the anger in his eyes. She turned quickly and left the barn, the gloves still in her hand.

John's mouth dropped open in surprise. As he stood staring at the empty barn doorway he felt the size of a very small bat.

Brownie had run for her bike to go home when Mary hurried out of the barn. "Can't you stay awhile?" Then she observed Brownie's downcast look. "What's wrong?"

she asked sympathetically. Her kind, freckled face invited confidence.

Brownie blurted out the whole story of how John hated her and she didn't know why and how everything she did seemed to make him hate her more.

"Has he hated you for a long time?" Mary asked.

"Ever since I've known him."

"Ever since you were kids?"

"I never saw him until this summer," Brownie explained.

"You mean this is the first time you ever saw your own cousin?"

"He's not my cousin and I don't know why he says he is. Our mothers were friends in college and John's staying with us because his grandfather is ill and his family couldn't go to Cape Cod like they planned. I've been as nice to him as I know how to be and he simply hates me."

"Isn't he ever friendly?" Mary inquired.

"Oh, yes, sometimes he is, especially when we talk about bats and science. But those are the two things I know least about in the entire world and so I can't talk very long," said Brownie sadly.

"Maybe you'd better learn about them."

"What I really like is English and history," objected Brownie.

"It was just a suggestion," Mary said and dismissed the

subject from her mind. She assumed Brownie had done the same. Suddenly a new idea occurred to her. "Do you have any brothers?"

"No, I'm an only child. Why?" Brownie asked.

"I was just thinking that John sounds like my brothers. Maybe the trouble is that you just aren't used to the way boys act when you live with them for twenty-four hours a day."

"How is that?" Brownie asked with great interest.

"Sometimes my brothers are friendly and fun and help me when I need them and really act like brothers should. And sometimes they're simply impossible and only act nice when they need my help."

"That sounds like John," Brownie agreed.

The conversation was interrupted by a great commotion in the barn. There were shouts of "Did you get any? How many? Quick, flip the net over." And then a loud, clear call rose above the commotion!

"Brownie, hurry up and bring my gloves."

Mary and Brownie grinned at each other and raced for the barn.

9.

THE EXCITEMENT and confusion in the barn were tremendous. John, with his hands safely encased in Mrs. Reese's driving gloves, helped Bill transfer the bats to the cage.

"Stand back," John shouted to the others as he picked up the first bat, "this one has rabies. He's shaking all over. Look at that mad snarl."

"Bill, you aren't going to take it back to the lab, are you?" Jimmy asked from a safe distance. "It'll give the disease to your other bats."

"Oh, gosh," Jack said from behind Jimmy's back.

"Do you suppose all our bats are rabid?" Mary wanted to know.

John's heart sank at that question. Suppose he had led Bill to a roost of rabid bats.

"What are you smiling about?" Brownie asked Bill.

[63]

The others had been so busy exclaiming over the rabid bat that they hadn't noticed Bill was listening.

"I'm smiling at what everyone is saying about this poor innocent bat," and he held out his arm to show them the bat which he held gently encased in his gloved hand.

Brownie and Mary gasped and backed away a few more steps.

"Do you know why he's really trembling and snarling?" Bill asked them.

"He's mad 'cause you caught him," was Jack's prompt reply.

"Frightened is more like it. You see this?" And Bill gently and expertly stretched out one of the thin, dark, cape-like wings. Even the girls drew nearer again. "It is one of the most delicate sense organs in the world. There is a network of nerves in this wing that is so fine and sensitive that any handling sets the bat aquiver. That's why he's trembling and snarling."

Later John offered to go back to the lab with Bill and help him unload the cage. Bill said he could do it alone but John insisted on helping. He was eager to see the inside of a laboratory in a big university. He found it was unlike any lab he had ever seen or even dreamed of. There wasn't a single microscope in it. It was just a big room with a battered desk and chair in one corner, a cage of bats, and an array of vertical wires strung on wooden frames which stretched from the ceiling to the floor.

[64]

"What do you do with all those wires?" asked John.

Bill smiled at John's curiosity and interest. "You know," he said, only half in jest, "if the funds for this project weren't already running low, I think I'd hire you as my assistant. You really are interested in science."

"Gosh, Bill," John said. "I'd work for free. All I need money for anyway is a new microscope and I'm already mowing lawns to earn that. I could help you whenever I'm not mowing."

John was hired on the spot. "Now you can tell me about those wires," he said.

Bill laughed. "I'll tell you all about them as we work. But first I need more bats. Do you suppose you could net more of those in that colony at the farm?"

"More bats!" John was amazed. The ceiling of the cage seemed to be jammed with bats hanging upside down.

"They aren't all good for the tests I'm making," Bill explained. "I need a steady supply of bats that are willing to fly in the lab. Some of these haven't turned out to be good fliers."

The days sped by after that eventful evening. John continued to mow lawns and store his hard-earned microscope money in the top drawer of the bureau in his bedroom. Welcome letters from his mother reported on the steady improvement in the health of his grandfather. The town tennis tournament would soon start and Brownie was busily getting her game in top shape. Between practice games she spent an unusual amount of time in her room where her mother assumed she was resting up for the next practice. The Reeses tried to encourage John to enter the tournament but he had something far more important to do than play tennis. He had his job in the lab.

At first John had had difficulty in carrying out his assignment to catch bats. But he had finally worked out a system with the help of Jimmy and Jack. He climbed the ladder first and reached out to the clump of bats with the net, nudged it until a bat fell in, and then quickly flipped the net over the rim and handed it down the ladder to Jimmy. Jimmy passed it down the ladder to Jack, who proudly stood on the barn floor and guarded the ensnared bat with heavily gloved hands. Then the three boys would manage to transfer the bat to a special bat-carrying box that John had drilled with tiny holes to let in air.

Two good things had come out of all this bat-hunting. One was that John had conquered his fear of heights. He was up and down the ladder so much that he no longer gave a thought to climbing to the top of the barn. The other was that Jimmy and Jack had become his very good friends. Their bat hunts were enormous fun.

John and Brownie didn't see too much of each other now, but when they did John was pleasant enough, and on the family's Sunday trips to the ocean he seemed to enjoy himself. Brownie even reported to her mother that every now and then he was a lot of fun. John never invited her to come to the lab though he did tell her something of the work he and Bill were doing. He didn't go into great detail about it because he figured that Brownie wouldn't understand him if he did. He explained it to her in the most elementary terms, though every now and then he couldn't resist showing off his newly-acquired knowledge of bats. Brownie seemed to him to understand what he said, but then she had always been a good listener.

He explained that bats caught insects and dodged trees and found their roosts in barns and caves by a system of echo-location. "You see," he said, "as the bat flies it sends out signals that you and I can't even hear. If these signals hit a bug, for instance, echoes bounce back to the bat and in that way he can figure out where the bug is. This system helps him find his roost, or dodge any obstacles, or fly wherever he wants to fly."

"In other words," Brownie said, "he uses sonar instead of his eyes."

"That's exactly it," John said with great surprise.

"What sort of project is Bill working on?"

"What he's doing is very complicated and you have to know all about sonar and radar and physics and all those things. But his work is part of a huge project which compares efficiency of a bat's echo-location system with that of systems which scientists and engineers have figured out."

[67]

One evening, many days after John had started working in the lab, he finally invited Brownie to ride to the farm with him to catch bats. Brownie accepted with pleasure. She would not have been so flattered by his invitation had she known the whole truth. He had invited her only after the Masons and Grandpa Hendricks had complained because he didn't bring his cousin with him.

10.

EVERYONE WAS HAPPY to see Brownie when she and John arrived at the Hendricks farm. Mary and Mrs. Mason hugged her, Grandpa said she hadn't grown more than an inch since he last saw her, and Jimmy and Jack grinned at all the goings on. Mrs. Mason said, "This calls for a celebration. I'll unplug the iron and fix some lemonade."

"You have a lot of washing and ironing to do, don't you?" Brownie said to Mrs. Mason when she returned to the back porch with the lemonade.

"The ironing isn't so bad but I must admit that the washing seems endless. Since my old machine broke down I've been washing the clothes by hand every day so they don't get ahead of me."

"Confound it, Louise," Grandpa said in a tone of voice that astonished Brownie, "I'm doing the best I can to get you a washing machine. But how's a man supposed to cure a crop of hay when it starts raining the afternoon he cuts it and keeps on raining for two weeks?"

"Dad," Mrs. Mason pleaded, "please don't worry about the washing machine. I'm sorry I mentioned it. Anyway, that's enough of our problems," she said. "Let's enjoy our celebration."

Brownie stayed on the porch with Mary while the boys went bat hunting. She was not going to butt in on John's bat hunt unless invited. In a short time familiar bat-catching shouts were heard from the barn, and soon the hunters emerged triumphant. Another bat lay quivering in the bottom of the box.

"Whew," John said, "I was beginning to think I wouldn't reach the bats this time."

"I think they're getting smart and moving away from the ladder," Jimmy said.

"Just remember," Grandpa said, "that when you get tired of catching bats with a net, I'll show you the real sporting way to do it."

"Show me now," John said. "Bill can always use more bats."

"Aw, not now," Jack begged. "Every night you promise to play high-over after you've caught your bats, and then you always have to go home or something. Brownie's here and we can have a good game."

"Go on and play high-over," Grandpa said. "There's time enough to show you how to catch bats when they begin to swoop around."

[70]

"Boys stand the girls," Jimmy yelled.

"That's unfair," Mary said. "There are only two of us."

"But there's no way to divide five evenly," Jimmy reminded her. Then he looked at Jack.

Jack saw the look. "Oh, no, you don't," he said quickly. "You're not pushing me on a team with a bunch of girls."

"Let's stand the boys," Brownie suggested to Mary. "We can probably beat them anyway."

"Brownie and I still don't know how to play," John reminded them.

"It's easy," Jimmy said. "First you start with a ball," and he held out a dilapidated old softball. "One team stands on one side of the smokehouse and the other team on the opposite side. Then you start throwing the ball over the smokehouse, and each time you throw you yell 'high-over.'"

Jack interrupted and concluded with what he thought was a perfectly clear explanation. "And if the other team catches the ball they chase the other team around the smokehouse and then the other team isn't on the same side of the smokehouse any more. See?"

"No," John said, "but I suppose I'll catch on as I play."

Jimmy got ready to throw the ball over the smokehouse. "Now, Jack, you watch around this corner and John, you watch around the other," he said.

"But what do I watch for?" asked John.

"It's this way. If Brownie catches the ball she'll come after us around one side and Mary will come around the

[71]

other. Only Brownie can tag us because she has the ball. Understand? You're supposed to see if the one coming around your side has the ball and if she does you tell us and we'll run the opposite way."

"Hurry up," Mary called.

"High-over," Jimmy shouted. He pretended to throw the ball hard, but really only lobbed it gently up on the roof so that it rolled back toward him. He caught it and winked at John.

"What are you doing?" John asked.

"This fools them," Jimmy said in a low voice. "Then they'll miss the ball when I really throw it."

"Quit your kidding and play," Mary called.

"High-over," he called again. This time the ball arched high in the air and over the smokehouse.

"Don't worry, they won't catch it," he said to John and Jack who were watching the corners.

"Brownie caught the ball," John yelled with surprise, and the three of them raced around the opposite side.

"Now I get it," John said, and the game continued amid much shouting by the boys and shrieking by the girls.

"I don't see why Brownie has to shriek all the time," John said to Jimmy after one particularly piercing cry.

"Don't pay any attention to it," Jimmy said. "All girls shriek."

"I'd never noticed it so much before."

"Don't you have a sister, John?"

He shook his head.

"That's why you haven't noticed it. They *all* shriek *all* the time."

"What are you doing, Grandpa?" Jack suddenly called. The old man was standing out in the yard throwing a white object into the air, picking it up when it fell to the ground, and throwing it up again.

"Catching a bat."

"What?" "How?" All the children asked questions at once and gathered around Grandpa.

"If I keep throwing this balled-up handkerchief into the air," he explained, "I'll fool a bat into thinking it's something to eat. He'll dive on it, get his claws caught in the cloth, and then I'll have him. Did it all the time when I was a boy. Used to throw pebbles too. And balls of cotton."

"Let's try it," Jimmy said. John had his doubts about whether a bat would be fooled by a handkerchief but it looked like a good game anyway. Soon the air was full of handkerchiefs, pebbles, shouts, and bats. Each time a bat careened toward them the girls shrieked and squealed.

"No wonder we couldn't catch a bat," John said later as he and Brownie rode home along the quiet, country road. "You shrieked so loud you scared them away. And Grandpa was disappointed."

"John, you know perfectly well that any noise I made

wasn't even close to upsetting the bats' ability to tell one sound from another. So I couldn't have scared them away." Brownie tossed her head and pulled her bike out in front of John.

John puzzled and frowned to himself. How did Brownie know her shriek wouldn't really jam the bats' signals? She didn't know anything about ultrasonic sound waves. Or did she? She hadn't been in the lab to hear Bill talk about that. He looked at the ponytail bouncing jauntily ahead of him. Was that girl really a scientist after all?

11.

BREAKFAST was over. Mr. Reese had gone to his office, John to the lab, and Brownie and her mother were washing the breakfast dishes. Suddenly the doorbell rang and Brownie came back from the door with a letter in her hand.

"Mother, it's a *Special Delivery* letter for John."

Mrs. Reese took it and read the return address. "It's from his mother and she's still with her father. I hope he isn't worse. Brownie," she said, "you must take this letter to John right away."

"Can't it wait till he comes home for lunch? He doesn't want me near that lab."

"Why would he possibly mind your coming to the lab, Brownie?"

"I don't know. But I just have a feeling he doesn't want me there."

"Brownie," her mother said with a slight touch of ex-

[75]

asperation in her voice, "I think you're letting your imagination run away with you. I've never known a nicer, more polite and pleasant boy."

"He's nice and polite and pleasant," Brownie said, "but do you know what he tells everyone about me?"

"Why, no. What in the world does he say?"

"He tells everyone he meets that I'm his cousin."

"Oh, Brownie," her mother laughed. "What is so wrong with being called his cousin? I think that's rather flattering."

"That's what I used to think," Brownie said, "but I talked to Mary about it, and she said that her grandfather was always quoting some old saying about how you can't help who your relatives are but you have the privilege of choosing your friends. And Mary and I think he tells everyone I'm his cousin because that means he can't help the fact that he has to be seen with me. You know, Mother, he really doesn't like me."

"Wasn't he nice to you on the trip to the farm last night?" her mother asked with some alarm.

"He was all right. But I just can't explain it. He sort of acts like he doesn't trust me, and he won't really let me get to know him. He won't let me be his friend."

"I'm very sorry," her mother said, shaking her head. "I had begun to think John was enjoying his summer with us. I'll take the letter to him."

"Oh, no, I'll take it," Brownie said with a shrug. "It

can't make matters any worse than they already are."

Brownie made her way through the science building to Bill's lab. There was a large sign on the door which read:

ATTENTION PLEASE
DO NOT OPEN DOOR
KNOCK BEFORE ENTERING

Brownie knocked on the door. There was no answer. She knocked louder. She could hear voices inside. She was trying to figure what to do with the letter when the door was cracked open a bit and Bill peered through.

"Brownie!" he said with surprise. "Come in quickly. I don't want the bats to escape."

Brownie slipped through the door quickly and Bill closed it. "It's your cousin," he called to John.

John was standing at the other end of the room with the insect net in his hand. "I see her," he said ungraciously.

"A *Special Delivery* letter just came for you and Mother thought you should have it right away." Brownie started to add that she hadn't wanted to come, that her mother had insisted, but this proved unnecessary. John's face had already flushed a deep red with well-deserved embarrassment over his rudeness.

"Oh, thank you," he mumbled as he tore open the envelope.

[77]

Brownie looked curiously around the lab. Five wooden frames were banked from one end of the room to the other. Threaded on these frames were an array of vertical wires. A bat was darting from one end of the room to the other, dodging in and out of the wires.

"Is that a *Myotis lucifugus* or an *Eptesicus fuscus?*" Brownie asked Bill.

"It's an *Eptesicus*," Bill said with surprise. "All of the ones I'm using now are the big brown bats from the Hendricks barn."

"Just so long as it's not a *Desmodus*." Brownie shivered.

"I wouldn't care to have to feed one of those," Bill joked.

"The natural sonar of the *Eptesicus* certainly incorporates unusual refinements." Brownie spoke slowly and with precision. "It's hard to believe that it can get through that maze of wires by means of its echo-location system."

"Then you already understand my project," Bill said, delighted to have such an intelligent, interested onlooker in his lab. "I have these wires spaced apart at only twice the bat's wingspan," he explained enthusiastically, "yet if you watch carefully you'll see that this one is able to get its signals back from each wire in time to avoid touching it. You see," he continued to his interested listener, "John and I keep a record of the hits and misses on the flight of each bat. After we've tested all of them with this wire, then we change to thinner wires and check the hits

[80]

and misses on those. We want to see how thin the wire has to be before the bats' sonar finally becomes ineffective."

"Very interesting," Brownie said, as if she understood every word of the short lecture. She was unaware of the fact that John had finished reading his letter and stood listening to her conversation with his mouth wide open. "*Myotis lucifugus, Eptesicus,*" he was repeating, "and how did she know a vampire bat was a *Desmodus?*"

"Why didn't you tell me that your cousin knew so much about bats?" Bill asked.

John was so puzzled he was speechless. Brownie became quite flustered.

"Mother wanted me to find out if there was any special news about your grandfather," she said to John.

"He's a lot better, thank you."

"Fine," and Brownie started for the door.

"Step out quickly," Bill called. "I don't want this bat to escape. He's a particularly good flier."

Brownie went to her room after lunch and read a book while John disappeared to write a letter.

DEAR MOTHER:
I got your letter today and I was glad to hear that Grandad thinks he's well enough to stay with a housekeeper so we can go to Cape Cod. I'm sorry you went to all the trouble to arrange for me to enter the Museum late because I really think you should stay with him

until he's well. Besides, Bill needs me. You know I told you in my last letter that I was helping Bill with his bats. Now I'm doing more than just catching and feeding them. I'm helping him test the efficiency of their echo-location system and then he's going to compare that with the radar and sonar that scientists and engineers have made. It's a real neat job.

Well, that's all for now and say hello to Grandad and explain to him why I can't go to Cape Cod.

Love,

JOHN

After John had addressed the envelope to his mother, he remembered that he owed Stevie a letter. He dashed off a short one.

DEAR STEVIE:

You asked in your letter if I was playing much tennis. I'm not because I'm helping the scientist I wrote you about. We caught lots of bats and now we're experimenting with them in his lab. It's real neat work. You know my cousin? She sure has changed a lot since I came. You wouldn't believe it. She's a good tennis player and she's in a tournament. She knows a lot of science for a girl. I've got to mail this letter so that's all for now.

Your friend,

JOHN

John started down the stairs on his way to the post office. "Hey, Brownie," he called.

"Yes," she answered from her room.

"Have time for a set of tennis after dinner?"

"With you?"

"Sure. Or won't you play with anyone but Tom Jackson?"

"Well, I—I didn't know," she stammered as she opened the door to her room. "You're always so busy, I mean, you know, lawns to mow and bats to catch and things like that."

"Can you play?"

"Yes." Brownie was dazed by the unexpected offer and by the first genuinely friendly smile she had ever been granted by John Stevens.

"So long then," he said and started off to the post office with the letters to his mother and Stevie. He whistled as he ambled down the walk.

12.

BROWNIE WAS SO HAPPY over the tennis date she could hardly settle down and eat dinner. John hardly ate either, but that was because he was so interested in telling Brownie and her parents about how he had helped Bill put finer wires in all the frames for to-morrow's flight tests.

"Bill surely was impressed today with what you knew about bats," John said to Brownie. Then he turned to Mr. Reese. "She even knows the species of bats and all about their sonar."

"Brownie!" Her father looked quite pleased. "This surprises me. Where did you learn all this?"

"Oh, Daddy." She flushed. "I don't really know very much. John's just being nice."

"No, I'm not," John insisted. "Bill said that even some of the students at the University weren't as well informed as Brownie. And I told him that you sure must have good schools here because the eighth-grade kids in my school weren't that smart."

Brownie looked as if she'd like to crawl under the table.

"I'm going to have to do some apologizing at the first PTA meeting in the fall," Mr. Reese said.

"Why?" Brownie was alarmed. She could sense that the conversation was getting out of hand.

"Because I've been quite outspoken in my criticism of the science curriculum. I've insisted that you children could grasp far more difficult subject matter than they were giving you. If what Bill says about your grasp of this sonar is true, then I've been unfair in my criticism of the school and I want to be the first to admit it."

"And if a girl who gets a C in science can impress Dr. Thomas," her mother said, "think what our A students must know."

Brownie looked at her plate, picked at her food, and turned a rosy red. She was saved from further misery by the ring of the front doorbell. "I'll go." She was grateful for the interruption.

"Bill! Come in."

"Am I interrupting your dinner?" he asked.

"You aren't interrupting a thing! We're glad to see you!"

Mrs. Reese came into the hall and invited Bill to join them for coffee and lemon meringue pie.

"That's my favorite kind of pie," he said.

"What's new at the lab?" John asked.

"That's what I came about. I was curious to see if the bats could successfully dodge those tiny wires we set up this afternoon. When I opened the cage to take out a bat, I found quite a few of them appeared to be unusually sluggish."

"Did I give them the wrong food? I thought you told me to give them that canned baby food today. Was I supposed to have fed them the meal-worm larvae?" an anxious John inquired.

"No. It's just that it's hard to feed them a proper diet in captivity. I've experimented with many foods, but nothing keeps them in top shape like the insects they catch for themselves."

"What'll you do?" Brownie asked.

"I was hoping John could go out to the farm and help me catch more bats. Then I can set the sluggish bats free."

"But I had asked Brownie to play a set of tennis," he protested.

Mrs. Reese looked surprised at this statement.

"We can play tennis another time," Brownie insisted. "The bats are more important."

"Your daughter certainly knows a lot about—" Bill started to say, but Brownie interrupted nervously.

"I don't mean to rush you, but the bats will be leaving the roost if you don't hurry."

"You're coming with us, aren't you?" John asked.

"Me? Sure, if you want me," Brownie said happily. As

she hurried from the dinner table she saw her mother's amused look. It hardly seemed possible that only this morning she had said, "You know, Mother, he really doesn't like me."

When Bill drove his old station wagon into the farm driveway, the Mason children stopped their game of high-over, Grandpa stopped rocking, and Mrs. Mason waved to them from under the clothesline.

"Going on another bat safari?" Grandpa asked waggishly as Bill and John unloaded the cage, the net, and two pairs of leather gloves.

Bill grinned good-naturedly and explained the feeding situation in the laboratory and the need for a successful hunt tonight if he was not to lose time on his research project.

"In that case I better help you," Grandpa said in all seriousness.

"But Grandpa, you can't climb the ladder," Jimmy and Jack said together.

"I can climb that ladder any day I want to," the old man said indignantly. "I'm still the man around this place."

The children were sorry they had wounded the old man's intense pride.

"But *I* don't have to climb ladders to catch bats," he added. "I out-think them."

"You mean you're going to try to catch them with a handkerchief?" John asked.

"What's that?" Bill wanted to know.

Grandpa explained how as a boy he used to tease the bats into diving on pebbles, handkerchiefs, and wads of cotton, and how they sometimes became ensnared in the handkerchief.

Bill laughed and said, "No wonder you think a net isn't the sporting way to catch bats, Mr. Hendricks, but I'd hate to have to depend on that method for supplying bats for my research project."

"We didn't even catch one little bat the other night," Jack reminded him.

"Didn't stay with it," Grandpa answered tersely. "You young folks just go on in the barn with all your paraphernalia and leave me out here with my handkerchief. And we'll see."

"I'll help you, Grandpa," Brownie said.

"Me, too," Mary said.

"It's like choosing sides for a game," Jack said excitedly, moving closer to Bill and the side he was choosing to play on.

The game was on: the net hunters versus the handkerchief hunters. Mary and Brownie were frantic in their effort to keep the handkerchiefs in the air.

"Easy," Grandpa cautioned. "We're going to have to do this for a spell."

The girls settled down and threw the handkerchiefs in the air with a quieter rhythm. "How's John acting?" Mary asked between tosses.

"Wonderful," Brownie said. "He even invited me to play a set of tennis with him."

There had never been better bat hunting in the Hendricks barn because there had never been such an efficient system for catching bats. Bill stood at the top of the ladder with the net. He nudged bats into the net, flipped the net over the rim, handed the net down the ladder to Jimmy, who passed it farther down the ladder to Jack. Jack gave the net to John, who emptied the bats into the cage and returned the net to Jack. He gave it to Jimmy, who handed it to Bill, who caught more bats and started them on their way down to the cage again.

They worked so quickly and efficiently that they had fourteen bats in the cage before the bats were thoroughly disturbed and awakened. "I hope we don't need any more bats," Bill said as they left the barn, "because they've moved so far over on the beam that I can hardly reach them."

"Caught any bats?" the net hunters called to the handkerchief hunters.

"We're in no hurry," Grandpa answered.

"May I join the handkerchief hunters?" Bill asked. "I've been wanting to try your system." He pulled a white handkerchief out of his pocket as he talked.

"Don't help their team," Jack complained. "We're ahead 14 to 0."

"Shut up," Jimmy whispered fiercely to Jack. "You

don't have to rub it in because we beat Grandpa's team."
A rabbit punch to Jack's upper arm helped reinforce his
order. Jack winced and glared at his big brother, but he
didn't discuss the one-sided score of the game further.

Soon the two teams had merged into one. Jimmy and
Jack threw up pebbles further to entice the bats in their
direction. The others threw up handkerchiefs. Excited
shouts and dipping and darting bats filled the air. Suddenly there was a mighty yell from John: "I've got one.
I've got one."

"I told you so, I told you so." Grandpa danced around
as spry as a boy. "I knew it would work!"

"Let it go, John," Bill shouted. "You don't have gloves on."

"But you need it in the lab," John argued, still clutching the snarling bat and the handkerchief.

"Don't argue, boy. Give it to me," Grandpa yelled sternly and snatched the bat from John's trembling hands.

13.

GRANDPA WAS ECSTATIC over the proof of his bat-catching theory. He had told these modern young scientists it would work! He tried to make light of his danger when he grabbed the handkerchief-ensnared bat from John. He held it in his bare hands until Bill had taken it from him with his gloved hand.

Grandpa was once more rocking in his favorite rocker on the back porch. Bill occupied a wicker chair. Jimmy, Jack, John, Mary, and Brownie were sitting with their legs dangling over the edge of the porch. Mrs. Mason brought a big pitcher of lemonade and joined the hunters for a well-deserved rest in the quiet and cool of the summer evening.

"Now, Grandpa," Bill said, "I'm not trying to say there's a very big chance these bats have rabies. But it is possible enough so I never take chances. And I don't want you or anyone else ever taking chances again for the sake of *my* research."

The familiar name "Grandpa" had slipped out without Bill's realizing he had said it. Grandpa didn't seem to mind. He harrumped and cleared his throat. "I figured a little old bat couldn't hurt a tough old codger like me and I didn't want John taking chances."

"But why didn't you let it go?" John asked.

"Now, now," Grandpa blustered, "Bill's got to get on with his research, hasn't he?" He kept on rocking. Finally he began to smile to himself and when at last he spoke it was in a mellow, reminiscent tone of voice.

"It's a good thing I didn't know about hydrophobia when I used to play with the bats that washed into the rain barrel."

"Tell us about it, Grandpa," the boys urged.

Grandpa loved to tell stories of his childhood and a back porch full of eager listeners was just what he liked. The fiddle-like music of the cicadas and katydids, and the steady croaking of the frogs in a nearby pond, furnished staccato sound effects for his story. "When I was a boy down in the southern part of the state," he began, tucking his thumbs under the straps of his overalls and leaning back in the rocker, "the bats used to be in the attic of our house something awful. Now you'd take a hard summer rain down there and let it keep up till evening and then you'd see some fun."

[95]

"But how?" Jack urged the storyteller on.

"You've noticed with all your bat hunting that they begin to creep out through the eaves of the barn toward evening. They did the same thing from our house. Only some of them would make the mistake of crawling up on the eave troughs that carried the rain to the rainspout. Now you remember I said that this all had to take place with a hard rain?"

Everyone nodded, even Bill and Mrs. Mason.

"Those poor bats would no sooner creep along the trough than they were caught up in the rushing water and swept right on down the rainspout and into the rain barrel."

"Couldn't they crawl out of the barrel?" Jimmy asked.

"They tried to but it was hard with their wet wings. Some of them could stay afloat with their wings spread out on the water like great big capes. So what I'd do," and Grandpa gave a chuckle, "was take a twig and hold it near the mouth of each bat that was trapped in the barrel. You should have seen them grab on when the twig touched their mouths. I'd lift them out of the barrel one by one and then rub their wings dry and stroke their heads."

"What'd you do that for, Grandpa?" Mary asked.

"I liked to. After a while they'd begin to hobble around on the ground using their wings like bent-up crutches. And then the fun really began. I'd see how close I could get my finger to their snarling mouths without getting bitten."

"Did they hurt you? Did they really bite?"

"Sure," Grandpa said in answer to the children's questions. "But I never gave it a second thought 'cause I didn't know they might give me hydrophobia. The strange thing was that a few of those bats acted friendly as if they wanted me to stroke their wings."

"Now, Father," Mrs. Mason chided gently. "The tale is getting quite tall."

"You're kidding us now, Grandpa," Mary said.

"I'm telling you the gospel truth," he insisted. "Every word I've said is fact."

"I believe Grandpa." It was Brownie who came to the old man's defense. "There's a Frenchman who's written a book about a bat that was his pet. The bat ate from his hand and liked to be petted. And I bet some of Grandpa's bats liked it too."

"Where'd you learn that?" John asked with great interest.

"I just happened to read about it." Brownie was suddenly evasive.

"Sounds like you've been busy," Mary whispered to Brownie.

"Sssh," Brownie answered, "don't let John hear you."

It was dark by the time the bat hunters drove back toward College Park. "I thought my grandfather was a good storyteller," John said, "but Grandpa is the greatest ever."

"We certainly have a good supply of bats," Bill said happily.

"I think the best thing about your research on bats is that it led us to the farm," Brownie said.

"It seems as if we've known them forever," John said, "and Grandpa isn't fooling me. He grabbed that bat to save me from a bite."

"And he held on to it for the sake of my research," Bill said. "His blustering doesn't fool me a little bit."

"You know," Brownie said, "everything would be perfect if Mrs. Mason didn't have to work so hard. She always looks so tired."

"It worries Grandpa that he can't buy a washing machine for her," John said.

When Bill stopped the station wagon in front of Brownie's house, John didn't get out immediately. He waited until Brownie had started up the walk. "Did you ever hear about the Frenchman and his bat?" he asked Bill in a low, hurried voice.

"Yes. There's a book about it. It's called *The Life of the Bat* and the name of the bat was Noctu."

John slipped out of the station wagon and followed Brownie up the walk. They sat down on the front steps of her house. It was too wonderful an evening to go inside. There were no frogs croaking as there had been out on the farm, but cicadas and katydids were in full voice and the fireflies hovered gently in the air as if suspended by magic. Brownie sat hugging her knees and thinking she would simply die from happiness. It had been the most wonderful day of her life.

"You know what I'm thinking?" John finally said.

"No. What?"

"What you said about how everything would be perfect if Mrs. Mason didn't have to work so hard," replied John.

"I know. And Grandpa's worried because he can't buy a washing machine for her."

John frowned. "He isn't likely to buy one soon because the hay crop was so poor."

"Do you know that if he hadn't grabbed that bat, you might have died of hydrophobia?" Brownie shivered at the thought.

"I wish he could buy the washing machine," John said.

"If I had enough money," Brownie said, "I'd simply give it to Grandpa to buy one. That's what I'd do. But all I have is thirteen dollars that Daddy gave me on my thirteenth birthday."

"I'm flat broke," John said, "except for the money I'm saving for the microscope."

There was a short period of thoughtful silence before Brownie said, "Maybe I can get a baby-sitting job and earn a lot of money and buy a washing machine."

"I'm the one Grandpa saved from getting hydrophobia, so I ought to buy it for him."

"But you don't have any money," Brownie reminded him.

"Of course I do. I have my lawn-mowing money."

"But that's for your microscope," Brownie reminded him.

"You know," John said, more to himself than to Brownie, "maybe Dad was right. Maybe my old microscope is good enough for a while." But he had said it aloud and Brownie had heard him.

"Oh, John, I've never heard of anything so generous. That's the most wonderful idea in the whole, wide world. It would really pay Grandpa back for saving you from dying of that dreadful disease."

John was a bit startled that Brownie had read his thoughts so accurately and raced ahead with his idea so quickly. But her genuine flattery was very pleasant. The wonderful night seemed made for grand plans, and giving up a long-desired microscope to buy a much-needed washing machine for someone else seemed a fine thing to do. Besides, there was no turning back. The plans were advancing too rapidly.

"Do you have enough money?" Brownie asked eagerly.

"I'll go see." John ran up to his room and collected all the lawn-mowing money he had been stuffing into his top bureau drawer. It looked like a huge amount when he first dumped the wad of crumpled bills and loose change on the dining-room table. But when he and Brownie had finished straightening out the paper money and sorting the change into piles, there didn't seem to be enough for a washing machine. No matter how many times they counted it, there were only thirty-six dollars on the table. John rubbed a hand over his stubble of blond hair and twisted his freckled face into a frown.

"How much do you suppose a washing machine costs?" he asked.

"I think it's more than a hundred dollars. I'll call the stores tomorrow and find out for sure," Brownie offered.

John estimated his future earnings. He had been in College Park four weeks and had made nine dollars a week by mowing three lawns. If he stayed four more weeks, that would make a total of only seventy-two dollars. That plus Brownie's thirteen dollars was still only eighty-five dollars. "I need more lawns to mow to make a hundred dollars."

"If you get more lawns to mow, you won't have time to help Bill. Let me get a lot of baby-sitting jobs," Brownie urged.

"If you do a lot of baby sitting, then you won't be able to practice and win the tennis tournament."

"Maybe the washing machine will only cost eighty-five dollars anyway," Brownie said, looking on the bright side. "I'll find out tomorrow."

John lay in bed that night adding and re-adding the money. Each time it came out to only eighty-five dollars. Suddenly a thought struck him that had nothing to do with the washing machine. I mustn't forget the name of that book, he thought to himself. He turned on the light, jumped out of bed, got a pencil and a piece of paper. He wrote: *The Life of the Bat.*

14.

"PRICING A WASHING MACHINE isn't as simple as you might think," Brownie announced to John the next day after she returned from her shopping trip. "The appliance store was full of them and every one had a different price and different features and all that. I had an awful time figuring out which one would suit Mrs. Mason." She and John studied the piece of paper on which she had written prices.

Wringer type	$ 72.50
Semi-automatic	
wringer type	127.00
Fully automatic	159.95

"There are lots of other washing machines," Brownie explained, "but the clerk helped me find the low, middle, and high-priced ones."

"Was this first one any good?" John asked hopefully,

indicating the lowest figure. "Because in three more weeks we'll have enough money for that."

"I imagined the wringer type went out with the old-fashioned days, but the clerk said some people prefer them and some don't have the proper plumbing for the automatic ones. What I thought," she continued, "was that we could ride out to the farm and ask Mary what kind her mother had before it broke down."

John's response was firm. "We'll ask Grandpa, not Mary. He's the one we're really buying it for anyway."

Later, as they rode toward the farm, John said, "I hope Grandpa's alone on the back porch."

"If Mrs. Mason is there I'll entice her into the house," Brownie offered, "so you can talk to Grandpa."

Everyone at the Hendricks farm seemed ready for John and Brownie's plan as if by some magical prearrangement. Grandpa was rocking on the back porch; Mary, Jack, and Jimmy were playing high-over; and Mrs. Mason was nowhere in sight.

"You go play high-over," John said excitedly to Brownie, "and tell them I'll be there in a minute."

"How's the young scientist?" Grandpa asked as John sat down on the edge of the porch near his rocking chair.

"Busy." John felt his pulse quickening as he searched for the grandest way to tell Grandpa they were going to buy a washing machine. Each time he started to speak, the words seemed inadequate to the occasion so he sat swinging his legs as he searched for the right beginning.

"Aren't you playing high-over this evening?"

"I'll play later," John said. Then he added: "I wanted to show you something first." He grinned as he handed Grandpa the piece of paper on which Brownie had listed the prices of the machines. He had suddenly abandoned the idea of a grand presentation speech. He'd creep up on the subject gradually.

"What have we here?" Grandpa asked genially. His lips moved as he read the list to himself. He began to knit his brows in puzzlement. John was so elated over the project that he failed to read the danger signs in Grandpa's expression. He didn't notice that Grandpa had stopped rocking.

"You needn't have bothered to price washing machines for me," Grandpa said brusquely. "I know perfectly well how expensive they are."

"But you don't know about our plan." John squared his shoulders. "We're going to buy the washing machine for *you*. We just came to check on which type Mrs. Mason used." John waited for Grandpa's expressions of surprise and gratefulness. But he waited in vain. He stopped grinning or swinging his legs over the edge of the porch. He was deaf to the happy shouts of the game of high-over. He was blind to the carefree darting of the bats in the evening sky. Somehow, in some way he could not yet comprehend, the wonderful plan had miscarried.

"Young man," the old man finally asked fiercely, "what gave you two the idea that I couldn't buy a washing machine for my daughter?"

John was so taken aback by the grim look on the face of his questioner that the answer tumbled out hurriedly. "Well, Grandpa, we saw how hard Mrs. Mason had to work doing the washing by hand and all, and we knew your hay crop wasn't good and you wanted to buy her a machine." John looked at Grandpa to see if his expression had softened. It hadn't, so he hurried on faster. "We counted the money I was saving for a microscope and that was thirty-six dollars and Brownie has thirteen dollars that her father gave her for her birthday. Brownie and I figured that in three more weeks I'll have mowed enough lawns to buy the one that costs seventy-two fifty."

Grandpa patted his foot on the porch floor. Finally, he cleared his throat and spoke slowly and proudly. "*I'm* the man of this house, and when there's a washing machine to be bought, I'll buy it." He resumed his rocking. John and the subject of washing machines were dismissed.

"But it's still daylight," Jimmy complained when John strode to the smokehouse and told Brownie it was time to go home.

"Please," Jack begged, "just one more game of high-over. You haven't even played yet."

"I have a lot of work to do tomorrow," John answered brusquely, and walked toward his bike. "And besides," he added, "how can you play a decent game with that dumb old ball? You ought to sew up the cover."

"What's chewing on him tonight?" Jimmy asked Brownie.

"Is he acting up again?" Mary wanted to know.

"No, he has a lot on his mind," Brownie explained. "We'll tell you later. It's a wonderful plan." She hopped on her bike and rode off after John.

"Was he surprised?" she asked John excitedly. "Which washer does he want to buy? What'd he say?"

"He said, *'I'm* the man of this house, and when there's a washing machine to be bought, I'll buy it.' "

"You mean he was mad? Won't he let us buy it? You mean he won't accept any help?" Brownie posed her incredulous questions all the way home. To all of them John answered with a wounded and disgruntled "Yes." His pride had received an almost mortal blow at the hands of the proud old man.

When Brownie and John reached home, they had a long talk on the front steps. Unlike the one they had held such a short, starry night ago, this was not full of happy, helpful plans.

"I think Grandpa's mean and selfish," Brownie said. "All he's doing is making Mrs. Mason work hard just because he's too proud to admit he needs help."

John found it comforting to have Brownie agree with him and defend the cause, even if it was a lost one.

"At least," she reminded him, "you'll still earn enough money for a new microscope."

The reminder that he could reach his original goal was small comfort to John, because in the meantime he had raised his goal higher. He had wanted to help someone else and he had failed. Grandpa wouldn't accept help.

As John was getting ready for bed that night, his eyes fell on the note he had written to himself the night before. *The Life of the Bat.* "I'll go to the library tomorrow and get that book," he thought before he went to sleep. "If Grandpa doesn't want any help that's all right with me. I'll spend the rest of the summer keeping up with Brownie and Bill on the subject of bats."

15.

ON HIS WAY to the Reeses' for lunch the next day John went by the public library to see if he could find a copy of *The Life of the Bat*. He searched the reference index. He looked under Bats. He looked under the N's to see if he could find the word Noctu. It was not there. He went back to the B's and jotted down the call number on one of the few books on bats. When he took his request to the librarian, she reported that the book was out on loan. He went back to the reference index and pondered over the few other titles on bats. He copied down the call number on the two books that sounded most interesting and informative. Again he was in for a disappointment, for these two had been checked out.

"This is interesting," the librarian said. "We've had these books on our shelves for a long time and they've had no circulation. Recently there seems to have been a considerable interest in bats. Maybe you'd like to leave your name and telephone number and I'll call you when the books are returned to circulation."

"I'll only be here for the rest of the summer," John explained, "and I was anxious to read about bats right now."

"In that case I'll see what I can do," the librarian said. "I'll check this number and see when the books are due back." She turned to a file and studied some cards. When she had finished she reported, "All the books are checked out to Brownie Reese."

"Brownie Reese!"

"Yes, and they're due back tomorrow," the librarian concluded with satisfaction.

John stumbled blindly out the library door. He was shocked and hurt. What a sneaky, mean thing to do! She didn't really know anything about bats. She didn't like science. She was cramming. She was just pretending to be smarter than he was. He grumbled and groused as he walked along. Just the time I'm nice to her and make plans and begin to trust her, she goes and does a dumb thing like this. He was sorry he hadn't gone to Cape Cod with his mother. He was sorry he had told Stevie that Brownie knew a lot about science. He was sorry he had said Brownie had changed a lot. She was just what he'd expected when he came. A girl cousin who would butt into everything and get in his way. His pride was wounded. He felt he had been fooled.

It didn't take John long to figure out a solution to the

whole unpleasant situation. He'd write his mother and tell her he wanted to spend the rest of the summer with her and his grandfather in Indiana. There was no point in staying in College Park, New Jersey, mowing lawns. Grandpa Hendricks didn't want his help anyway. He'd write his mother a letter and mail it today and he bet anything he'd be out of this little old hick town in a week. Girl scientist indeed!

"Hi!" Brownie called from the front door as John strode up the walk. He grunted and stalked by her with his head down. "Now what in the world's got into him again?" she wondered, then quickly answered her own question. He was still mad at Grandpa for being so selfish and upsetting their plans.

John went straight to his room and started to work on the letter to his mother. He had finished it and addressed the envelope by the time lunch was ready. He planned to mail it before he went back to work. Once again his careful plans were doomed to go awry.

"John, you had a telephone call from Mr. Hendricks," Mrs. Reese said when he came into the kitchen for lunch. "He wants you to call him."

"Now what does he want?" John said ungraciously as he walked toward the phone in the hall.

"Is something bothering John again?" Mrs. Reese asked.

"I'll tell you about it later," Brownie answered. In

[113]

answer to her mother's worried look she added, "This has to do with Grandpa Hendricks. There's nothing wrong between John and me. He's finally treating me like a friend."

"I'm relieved to hear that."

"What'd Grandpa want?" Brownie asked when John returned to the table. She was consumed with curiosity.

"He wants to see me right away." John put his head down and ate his lunch.

John had no idea why Grandpa felt it was so important to see him. Certainly he had sounded pleasant enough on the phone, which was more than could be said for his tone of voice the night before. He had promised Grandpa he'd bicycle out to the farm immediately after lunch. He had planned to mail the letter to his mother but he forgot about it in his puzzlement over the telephone conversation. It lay on the desk in his room.

Jimmy and Jack were surprised to see John arrive at the farm in the middle of the day. "Hey, what's wrong?" was their immediate question. "Lose all your bats?"

Grandpa put his head out the barn door. "Skedaddle and finish your chores," he said to the two boys. "John's come to see me."

"Aw, Grandpa." The boys looked puzzled and hurt but they disappeared from sight.

Grandpa invited John into the barn and motioned for him to take a seat on one bale of hay, while he lowered himself stiffly onto another. John nervously fingered the twine which bound the bale on which he was sitting. His eyes followed the path of the long ladder to the top of the barn. The familiar colony of bats still clung beneath the rafter, but by now it was securely out of reach of the insect net.

"John," Grandpa said, "I've been thinking."

"Yes, sir."

"You know one thing I've been thinking about?"

"No, sir." John studied the laces on his sneakers.

"Your offer of a washing machine."

John began to fidget and pick out bits of hay from the bale. He was sure Grandpa was building up to another blast. He didn't dare look at him.

"I've been thinking about something else."

"Yes, sir."

"I've been thinking that I've been a pretty selfish and stubborn man."

"Yes, sir!" John agreed heartily before he thought and then added desperately, "I mean, no, sir."

"You were right the first time," Grandpa said. "I was thinking of myself and not my daughter. I'd like to accept your generous offer of a washing machine. Do you and Brownie really have enough money to buy one?"

John was not prepared for this unexpected shift in events. Last night he had confidently anticipated this acceptance of their offer. But now it was too late. He

[115]

was leaving town. He wasn't getting involved in good deeds any more. He sat plucking at the hay and trying to figure out how to tell Grandpa that he and Brownie were no longer partners. The offer of the machine had expired. He was leaving town.

"Psst, John," came a loud and unexpected whisper from outside the barn. "Answer Grandpa's question."

Grandpa and John looked up just in time to see Jack duck behind the barn door.

"Jack!"

"Yes, Grandpa," a meek voice answered.

"Jimmy!"

"Yes, Grandpa," another meek voice replied.

"If you two are that curious to listen, you might as well have a seat in here where you can hear."

"Yes, sir!" and the two boys hurried in, confident that Grandpa would have a teasing twinkle in his eye.

Once more John's plans were taken out of his hands and swept merrily along beyond his control. This time Jimmy and Jack joined in to upset his scheme for leaving town and abandoning forever his cousin and his good deeds. They simply took over the discussion and before John could get a word in edgewise, he seemed to be in partnership with the old man and Brownie.

"So that's what you were talking about last night," Jimmy said. "That's the neatest idea I ever heard. Won't Mother be surprised? Now she won't be so tired. Boy, you and Brownie are some friends. Do you really have enough money? If you don't have enough, why don't you let Grandpa help too? He has forty dollars saved for the washing machine already. Don't you, Grandpa?"

By the time John returned to College Park he and Grandpa had made careful plans to buy the washer that cost one hundred and twenty-seven dollars. John would have to earn thirty-eight more dollars, and this, added to the thirty-six he already had, Grandpa's forty, and Brownie's thirteen, made it all possible. John tore up the letter he had written to his mother about joining her at his grandfather's house. He would have to keep on mowing lawns in College Park. He must endure Brownie Reese.

16.

THE LATENESS of the hour at which John returned to the lab after lunch and the woebegone expression on his face made it only natural that Bill should ask, "Something wrong, fellow?"

"I'll say. Nothing ever works out right for me. Every single time I make plans, something always happens. It seems as if I'm jinxed."

It didn't take much sympathizing on Bill's part before John told him all about the plans to go to the Cape Cod Junior Museum of Natural History for the summer and how those plans were upset. Then he told him about buying a washing machine and how Grandpa had gotten mad at him.

"He's a proud old man," Bill said, "and I'm not a bit surprised at his reaction."

"That isn't the end of the story," and John described Grandpa's sudden change of mind and their latest plans for jointly buying the semi-automatic, wringer-type washer.

"I think that's an excellent solution. How much money do you have?"

"Brownie has thirteen dollars, Grandpa has forty, and I have thirty-six, and it costs one hundred and twenty-seven. I only make nine dollars a week mowing lawns, so that means I have to change my plans again and stay around here for the rest of the summer if we're ever going to pay for it. And there's no way out of it."

Bill was considerably confused by John's reasoning. He didn't understand why it was such a hardship for John to remain for the rest of the summer and help Grandpa pay for the washer, when he had already been planning to stay around and pay for most of it by himself. "Is a summer in College Park that unpleasant?" he asked.

John answered grimly: "It's not so good." Then he hurried to add, "Except for working with you in the lab. That's made up for missing out on the museum."

"Whew. I'm glad you added that. I was just about to ask you a big favor. It has to do with the lab," Bill hastened to add.

"What's that?"

"I wondered if you could possibly persuade your cousin to come to the lab and help us."

"Brownie!"

"I know it's quite a bit to ask." Bill completely misinterpreted the tone of John's shocked voice. He hastened to explain why he needed extra help. Today he was going to start experiments to find out whether or not he could "jam" the bats' system of echo-location. He was so enthused over this part of the experiment that he told John all about it without pausing to notice that his usually avid listener looked as if he had been poisoned.

"You see," Bill explained, "so far we've looked upon the echoes which the bats get back from these wires as isolated sound waves. Actually this isn't true, even in the lab, and it certainly isn't true in nature. Every time a bat is trying to catch an insect, its ears receive a whole host of sounds in addition to the faint echoes from the insect. These are echoes from close-by trees, leaves, twigs, and blades of grass.

"Now the big question is how the bats can discriminate between a faint echo that means food and a competing one that means a leaf. However they do it, we have to admit they are highly proficient. I'm curious to see if I can upset their system. I plan to generate artificial sounds in here so that extra noises are added to the echoes coming back to the bats from the wires, the floor, and the walls. In other words, I'm going to see if I can jam or confuse their signals. I could use an extra pair of hands to operate the loud-speaker and generate special high-frequency sounds. I thought that since Brownie was so interested in bats and knew so much about them, that she was the natural one for the job."

"She's scared to death of bats," John reminded Bill emphatically.

"That's all right. You and I will handle the bats and she can handle the loud-speaker. We'll make quick work of this experiment. Then I'll have ample time to prepare all my conclusions and reports before school starts again."

John was in a tight spot. He appreciated the fact that Bill needed help and he hated to let him down. But Brownie Reese in his lab! After the way she had cheated on what she really knew about bats! He had one last ace up his sleeve and he played it desperately. "She isn't interested in bats. She's only putting on a big act. All she's been doing is cramming up on library books during the last couple of weeks and pretending she's smart."

This statement didn't have the desired effect at all. It only impressed Bill even more with Brownie's ability. "I teach undergraduates who cram for more than two weeks in the library and they don't learn as much as Brownie apparently has learned about bats in this short time. Anyway," he concluded, "you can't blame a girl for trying to be as smart as her cousin."

John gulped at this. Now he was sorrier than ever that he had claimed Brownie for a cousin. Bill was acting as if it were something to be proud of, instead of something a guy couldn't help. There was absolutely nothing he could do but nod and mumble a promise to ask Brownie if she would please come to the lab and help.

By late afternoon John had worked himself into a state of despair over having to *invite* Brownie into the lab with him. His chin sagged and his downcast eyes followed the toes of his sneakers slowly up the sidewalk toward the Reese home. Suddenly his freckled face came up and faced the waning day with hope. Brownie wouldn't be able to help in the lab! The tennis tournament wasn't over and she wouldn't want to forego the chance of winning.

Of course John had no sooner entered the house than Brownie bombarded him with questions about why Grandpa had wanted to see him. She was so complimentary and enthusiastic over the agreement he and Grandpa had made to buy the washer together that he didn't tell her it was really Jimmy and Jack who had worked it out.

"Say, Brownie." John sounded more nonchalant than he felt. "Bill had some silly notion today that you could come in the lab and help us with the bats. But I'll be glad to explain that you'll be busy winning the tennis tournament."

"Did Bill really want me to help him?" Brownie's brown eyes fairly sparkled and John tried to ignore them as he talked.

"I know you don't want to give up your tennis match, Brownie."

[122]

"I'll play the matches," she said. "I just won't take time to practice. That'll give me a lot of time to help."

"But if you don't practice, you'll lose."

"If I lose, Tom Jackson is a sure bet to win the tournament. And that would be all right with me," Brownie assured him.

"Tom Jackson win! That lousy player!" He made one final noble effort at saving a hopeless situation. "You know how you shriek when bats come near you? In the laboratory they're flying and zooming and dipping all over the place and they'd scare you to death." John balled up his fist into a bat and tore around putting on a first-rate demonstration of a loose bat getting into Brownie's hair. The effect of this heartfelt performance was the exact opposite of John's intention. She shrieked with laughter.

"Oh, John. You're the funniest bat I ever saw and I promise I'll never shriek again."

17.

BROWNIE HAD GIVEN UP trying to understand John. Although they had been working together in the lab since the day he had unwillingly brought her the message that Bill needed her help, John spoke to her only when it was necessary. He was acting exactly as he had when he first came to College Park in June—polite but not friendly. He congratulated her when she won the tennis tournament, but he was quite formal about it. Brownie talked the situation over with her mother and this time even she was unable to see any reason for John's behavior. There was really nothing for him to be worried about. The health of his grandfather continued to improve steadily. The washing machine was almost paid for, and the man at the appliance store had scheduled it for delivery the week John planned to make the final payment.

The work in the laboratory progressed with a speed that exceeded Bill's fondest expectations. He had finished the flight tests with the ever-decreasing sizes of wires and had the hits and misses of the bats on each size recorded and ready for analysis. He was busily piling up statistics on the bats' ability to distinguish important echoes from the distracting sounds he was generating in the lab. He and John had threaded wires one millimeter in diameter in the panels and spaced the wires eighteen inches apart. Both bats they had tested so far had been able to dodge the wires despite the fact that the loud-speaker Brownie was operating was filling the room with a noise field about the intensity of the bats' signals.

Bill had never known such dedicated or such solemn helpers as Brownie and John. They never smiled or joked together. Every now and then he'd say, "You two are working too hard. Why don't you take time off for a game of tennis? You're beginning to take *my* job too seriously."

In the end it was Bill who took time off for fun and not John and Brownie. There was a loud pounding on the lab door one Friday afternoon in August. It was Bill's former college roommate on his way to the seashore. He was so shocked at Bill's pallid face that he urged him to get away from the lab and his bats to join him for a Saturday in the sun. Bill insisted that he couldn't go, but Brownie reminded him that he had just told them his work was ahead of schedule. John offered to come into the lab in the morning and check on the bats. Brownie said she'd feed the bats their meal worms.

Bill was pleased and laughed at that. "I can't decline such offers. I'll go to the beach."

Even John managed a grin at the thought of Brownie holding a bat in one hand, trying to stuff a meal worm past its sharp teeth with the other. "I'll be back tomorrow night," Bill said as he left.

Saturday morning John and Brownie were at the lab early. They wasted no time in putting on leather gloves, placing the bat cage on the table, getting the meal-worm larvae and tweezers, and setting to work. The responsibility for the welfare of the bat colony weighed a bit heavily on John's shoulders and though he would not have admitted it, he was glad to have Brownie around to talk to and share the responsibility.

The bats were sluggish when John first picked them off the screen wire on the roof of the cage. He handed one to Brownie and got another for himself. He held it gently and stroked its furry head until it roused. Brownie held hers at arm's length. Her hand shook when it threw open its mouth and began to chitter excitedly, its white, needle-sharp teeth clearly visible.

"At least there's no trouble getting it to open its mouth for food," she said bravely.

"That's the easy part," John said. "The hard part is

[126]

getting it to swallow the worm." He picked up a worm with tweezers and put it way back in the bat's mouth.

"No wonder Bill has to set the bats free after a while," Brownie said after repeated efforts at trying to get her bat to swallow food had failed. "This one is going to starve to death."

"You almost have to force the worm down their throats with the tweezers. They don't like their food this way," John explained. "They're used to finding it in the air by echo-location."

"Would they like the worms better if we threw them in the air right here in the lab?" Brownie asked.

John started to discount the suggestion just because Brownie had made it, but his love of scientific exploration got the better of him. And anyway, it sounded like fun. "We could try it," he agreed.

At first the bats refused to fly. Each time John threw them into the air they flapped along half-heartedly until they got to the wall and then tried to cling to it. Failing that, they'd slide down on the floor and begin to hunch themselves along on their bent wings, screeching and complaining all the while.

"I was about to think they'd never orbit," John said when at last the two bats were dipping and flying around the lab.

"Grandpa would think this was the sporting way to

feed them," Brownie said as she tossed the first worm into the air.

"It got it. What a catch!" John yelled excitedly. One of the bats had streaked through the air and snapped up the worm before Brownie's throwing arm had returned to her side.

"I wonder why Bill never fed them this way," Brownie said. "It's a lot more fun."

Feeding the bats turned into a game. Brownie and John took the bats from the cage two at a time and threw worms to them. That way they could be sure each bat was getting its share. "This does take more time than stuffing the worms down their throats," John finally admitted.

"We can report to Bill that there's nothing wrong with their system of echo-location," Brownie said.

"I've got to get a drink of water," John panted. "This is hard work." He hurried from the room with his mind so concentrated on his thirst that he forgot the one cardinal rule of the lab: always close the door. He was bending over the water fountain in the hall when Brownie shrieked,

"John! Shut the door! Quick!"

"Oh, my gosh!" John raced for the door. He was too late. He met one of the bats zooming out of the lab and into the hall. Another whizzed over his head as he slammed the door. He turned back into the hall to pursue

the bats. Once more he was too late. They had disappeared from sight.

When Brownie came out of the lab, John said to her, "That's the dumbest thing I ever did. There's no telling where they're hiding."

"Maybe they went in here," and Brownie pointed to another lab.

"Just my luck that the door to the biggest lab in the science building is open," John moaned as he peered into the vacant lab.

There had never been such a thorough search for a bat. John and Brownie looked inside cabinets, they stood on chairs and searched on top of the cabinets. They pulled the window shades up and down at least a dozen times. They looked under the tables and under the microscope covers. "I'm glad no one's around here to see us," John said as he peered down the drain of the sink.

"Here's one of them," Brownie shouted, "down behind the radiator."

The search for the second bat was resumed with renewed vigor. "If we found one, we can surely find the other," they kept assuring each other. But finally Brownie admitted, "I give up," for not even the dusty radiators revealed the second bat.

"But we can't give up." John sounded desperate. "Bill needs every bat he has to finish the project and I hate to have to tell him that I forgot and left the door open. How dumb can a guy be!"

"In that case we'd better come back after lunch and look some more," Brownie said. "Maybe it will have come out of hiding by then." But the search after lunch was not fruitful either. The whereabouts of the bat remained cloaked in mystery.

"Why don't we go out to the farm and catch another bat to replace this one," Brownie suggested.

"That clump of bats in the barn has moved so far over on the beam that I can't reach it with a net."

"Maybe it's moved back toward the ladder. We haven't been out there for ages."

John chose to ignore this last statement. "I suppose it's worth a try," he agreed half-heartedly. "But we don't have much time. Bill will be back tonight."

18.

HAPPY, EXCITED SHOUTS greeted Brownie and John when they rode up to the Hendricks farm in the early evening. Jimmy, Mary, and Jack all began to talk at once.

"We knew you were coming."

"We just tried to call you."

"The washing machine came. We covered it up and made Mother promise not to peek. Let's show it to her now."

"It was supposed to be delivered next week," was John's brief answer.

Jimmy noticed the bat-catching paraphernalia loaded on the two bikes.

"Need more bats?" he asked.

"One," John answered and told them of the escaped bat.

"Is Bill going to be mad when he comes back tonight?" Jack asked.

"He's too nice to act mad," John said, "but he needed every bat in the colony to finish his experiment and I feel plenty stupid about letting one fly right out the door."

"Howdy," Grandpa called from the back porch. John told him his problem.

"Glad to see you again," Mrs. Mason called from the clothesline. John told her about leaving the door of the lab open and letting the bat escape.

"With all the bat catchers we have here," Grandpa said, "it looks as if we ought to be able to outsmart one bat."

"Shall we all throw up handkerchiefs?" Mary asked.

"First, I'd like to try and net one of those in the barn," John said, "and if that doesn't work we'll have to try Grandpa's way." John knew before he climbed the ladder that he'd never be able to reach the clump of bats with the net. But he felt better for trying. Meanwhile, he had more help from below than he cared for.

"It would take a giant to reach them," Jack called.

"Maybe you can stir them up so they'll begin to fly," Brownie called, "then we can start to throw handkerchiefs."

"You won't make it," Mary said as John held out the net toward the clump of bats hanging under the beam.

"Missed by a mile," Jack said.

While everyone was calling to John, Jimmy had disappeared. He returned with a long stick and started up the ladder. "Stir them up with this," he said to John, "and I'll take the net and try to catch one if it swoops toward us." But luck was not with them. When John nudged the bats with the long stick, they complained and squeaked and crawled over each other sluggishly. With more persistent prodding they only crept along the beam and disappeared under the eaves.

Everyone was discouraged but Jack. "Now we have time for a game of high-over," he suggested brightly.

"Don't you ever think of anything but high-over?" John asked.

"You haven't played in a long time."

"We've all got to help catch a bat," Jimmy reminded him.

"They're not flying yet," Jack persisted.

"All right," John agreed. "We'll play until we see the first bat flying."

Jack volunteered to be on Brownie and Mary's team before Jimmy suggested it.

"Gosh," John said when he saw the ball, "haven't you fixed that cover yet?"

"It's so loose now that it makes the game fun and dizzy," Mary answered. "Wait'll you see it."

Sure enough, the flapping cover made the ball spiral in crazy patterns back and forth across the smokehouse.

"High—high-over," Jimmy called, and threw the ball as high into the air as he could.

"You're cheating," Jack yelled. "We can't throw it that high when it's our turn."

While Jack was complaining and Jimmy and John were smiling self-satisfied grins over their high throw, Brownie caught the ball, raced around the smokehouse, and tagged both John and Jimmy with the grins still on their faces.

"Bat over head!" Grandpa called from the porch. The game of high-over came to a dead halt and the players scanned the evening sky for bats.

"Wouldn't you know they'd fly high tonight?" John moaned. "We'll never get them to dive on a handkerchief from way up there."

"There's no use trying yet," Jimmy said. "We might as well wait until they come down."

"Grandpa's already at work," John said, "so I'll go too. You all keep on with the game until the bats come down closer."

Grandpa and John stood with gloved hands and threw handkerchiefs in the air while Jack and Jimmy teamed up against Mary and Brownie in a game of high-over.

"Try to make the ball fall near Mary," Jack whispered to his big brother. "Brownie can catch anything."

"Is Mary this way or that way?" Jimmy said, pointing to the right and then the left.

[135]

"Hey, Mary," Jack called.

"What?"

"She's that way," Jack whispered, pointing to the left, the direction of the answer. "Never mind," he called to Mary.

"Let's switch sides," Mary called softly to Brownie. "They're up to something."

"High-over," Jimmy called, and feebly tossed the ball up on the smokehouse roof. "Not quite," he called as the ball wobbled down the roof and bounced off into his hand.

"Get ready for a high one," Mary said to Brownie.

"High-over!" and Jimmy tucked the loose cover and string around the ball, did a deep side twist, wound up, and shot the ball high into the air, over the roof and toward the corner of the smokehouse where Mary was supposed to be standing. By the time the ball reached the peak of its arched flight the cover had unfurled. A bat, flying high and sending out its signals for a juicy insect, caught the echoes from the ball and with unerring instinct dived on it as it headed earthward.

"Look!" Jack shouted, "that crazy bat thinks the ball's a bug."

"Hey, John," Jimmy called excitedly. "Come quick. We've got a bat flying in low."

"It's caught in the ball. It's coming down," Mary shrieked.

"I've got it," Brownie yelled.

[136]

"How'd you get over on that side?" Jimmy asked. "That was supposed to be Mary's ball."

"Let it go," John shrieked frantically as he raced toward Brownie. "You don't have gloves on. Let it go!"

But Brownie clutched doggedly at the ball and bat until John took them from her with his gloved hands.

"You got your bat! You got your bat!" Jack danced up and down. "Now aren't you glad I thought of playing high-over? I'm the one who outsmarted the bat."

"Aren't you glad we never sewed the cover up?" Mary asked. "The bat got caught in the loose string."

"Did it bite you?" John asked Brownie anxiously.

"I didn't feel it." She examined her hands carefully. "And I don't see any marks."

"That was a crazy thing to do," John scolded. "You know Bill told us not to take chances with rabies for the sake of his research."

"I wasn't taking chances for the sake of his research," she said quietly.

"Then why'd you do it? Just to win a game of high-over?"

"No," Brownie answered, looking John straight in the eye, "because you were so worried about letting the bat escape from the lab that I wanted to help you. And this time I didn't shriek. You did."

19.

JOHN WAS so surprised by Brownie's answer that he stood dead still and stared straight back at her. As the full meaning of her sacrifice became clear to him and he realized the danger she had willingly faced for his sake, he lowered his eyes and seemed lost in a study of the bat in his hand. The silence was intense.

"I'll tell you what," Grandpa finally said, "I'll take the bat now that you've caught it and put it in your box." He took the bat in his gloved hand and left.

"What I don't understand," John finally said to Brownie with a puzzled twist to his face, "is how you can be so sneaky one minute and such a friend the next."

"What do you mean?" Mary asked furiously. "You're a great one to talk about someone being sneaky."

"You stay out of it," Jimmy said to his sister.

For once Jack didn't say anything. His head turned

from one speaker to the other as if he were watching a tennis match.

"Yes, what do you mean?" This time Brownie was John's questioner and her ponytail bobbed belligerently. "When have I been sneaky?"

"You sneaked books on bats out of the library and put on a big act to Bill about what a great scientist you were and you pretended to be interested in echo-location and sonar and species of bats."

"How'd you know I got books out of the library?" Brownie asked, her face flushing crimson.

"Because I went to the library to borrow them and they were loaned out to you."

"She wasn't sneaking and she wasn't putting on a big act," Mary stanchly defended Brownie. "She felt sorry because you didn't get to Cape Cod and she was trying to be nice to you and make you happy and you were never nice to her unless you were talking about the bats in that old laboratory. She was just trying to learn about bats because that was all you seemed interested in. And I'm the one who suggested that she learn about bats, so if anyone was sneaky, it was I and not Brownie. So there!"

John was so overwhelmed by this long expression of feminine outrage that "oh, I didn't understand" was all he could say in his own defense. He wished he could bring a halt to the entire conversation, but he had started it and there was no stopping it now.

"Well, there's something *I* don't understand." Brownie was mad. "Why did you tell everyone I was your cousin?"

"Talk about sneaky," Mary said.

"Another secret!" Jack exclaimed.

"Aren't you cousins?" This time even Jimmy was astonished.

"Not exactly," John admitted. Seeing the puzzled and accusing looks on the faces around him he hastened to explain: "You see, Brownie's mother and my mother have known each other forever and I figured we were almost cousins."

"Why'd you go to all the trouble to figure that out?" Jimmy asked. "I don't get the point."

"To tell you the truth," John answered, "I don't either."

"If you aren't cousins," Jack wanted to know, "and you aren't almost cousins, then what are you?" He was always annoyed when he couldn't understand what was going on.

"I hope we're friends," John answered quietly. This time when he looked at Brownie there were no blushes and no lowered eyes. Instead, they began to grin at each other.

"Hello, there!" a voice called.

"It's Bill," Jack shouted. "Hey, guess what just happened?" He raced toward Bill so he could be the first one to tell him the news about the exciting capture of the bat. The others came on the run and they all laughed and talked at once. Bill stood shaking his head in amazement at the way the bat was caught in the loose cover of the ball.

"Are you sure it didn't bite you?" he asked Brownie.

"Positive," she answered and showed him her hands. "But I promise I won't ever do it again—even for a friend."

"Now," Bill said mysteriously, "I have a bit of news for John."

"What?"

"Anyone interested in lemonade and cookies?" Mrs. Mason called from the back porch.

"I'm afraid we can't wait, thank you," John answered. "It's getting dark and Mr. and Mrs. Reese will be worried."

"I told them I'd put your bikes in the station wagon and take you home," Bill said.

"Why were you talking to Mother and Daddy?" Brownie asked.

"Is that how you knew we were here?" John wanted to know.

"Let's have the lemonade and cookies first," Bill insisted.

But the children teased so for the bit of news that after one sip of the lemonade he had to give in and tell them. Even Grandpa was sitting on the edge of his rocking chair, and Mrs. Mason stopped to hear the news before she returned to her work.

"Guess who was waiting outside the door for me when I got back to the lab tonight?" Bill asked.

"My mother and father," Brownie guessed.

"Wrong."

"Another college roommate," was John's guess.

"Wrong."

"A colony of bats," Grandpa said, chuckling at his own joke.

"You're getting warm," was Bill's surprising answer.

"We give up. Tell us," everyone begged.

"When I got back from the beach, I went straight to the lab. It was getting dark and as I walked down the hall of the science building, there was a sudden swish, and a bat dived at me."

"The bat I let out?" John shouted.

"Did you catch it?" Jimmy asked.

"Sure. Then I tried to telephone John to see what had happened. Mrs. Reese told me how worried he was about the bat so I hurried out here to tell him that he hadn't lost a bat after all."

"We could have played high-over all the time," Jack complained.

"All that chase for nothing," Jimmy said.

"I'm not so sure it was for nothing," John said, looking at Brownie.

Mrs. Mason went back to her work and left everyone else drinking lemonade, eating cookies, and trying to solve the mystery of where the bat had been hiding while Brownie and John looked for it. Finally they gave up completely and admitted it would have to remain an unsolved mystery.

"When can we tell Mother about the washing machine?" Mary asked.

"Let's show it to her now," Jimmy said, "while we're having a sort of a party."

"No," John said. "I think we'd better be going. You can show it to her after we leave."

"Jimmy's right," Grandpa insisted. "Brownie's given her birthday money and you've mowed lawns all summer. We'll show it to her while you two are here."

"All right," John agreed reluctantly, "but you've got to tell her about it, Grandpa. We bought it for you to give her."

Everyone gathered in the laundry room around a mysterious-looking object covered by a sheet. Mrs. Mason was thoroughly mystified by the proceedings and the children were so eager for Grandpa to start the unveiling ceremony that they giggled and nudged each other as they stole glances at Mrs. Mason. Even Bill couldn't conceal his excitement.

Mrs. Mason was so overcome with surprise when Grandpa made his speech and removed the sheet from the gleaming white washing machine, that she stood smiling and dabbing at her eyes with her apron. First she thanked

Brownie, then Grandpa. "John," she finally said, "when I think that you gave up your new microscope to do this for our family, I just can't find words to thank you."

"Speech, John. Speech," Jimmy said mischievously. Jack, Brownie, and Mary joined him in demanding another speech.

This was the last thing in the world John wanted to do,

and he could gladly have pushed Jimmy into the laundry tub for thinking of it. But there was nothing to do but rise to the occasion and make a speech. "You all are the nicest friends I've ever had and this has been the best summer of my entire life."

"Even better than Cape Cod would have been?" Brownie asked hopefully.

"Much better," was John's emphatic answer.

"Will you be going home the minute the washing machine is paid for?" Jimmy asked.

"Not unless the Reeses make me," John said.

"They won't," Brownie said quietly.

"Then we can have a lot more games of high-over," Jack concluded happily.

"There's one thing about you, Jack." John laughed. "You don't give up. I promise I'll play high-over with you, but I have a lot of other things to do, too."

"Like what?" Jack insisted.

"Brownie and I have to help Bill finish his project. I have to read the books Brownie has taken out of the library on bats. I still don't know about that bat, Noctu."

"I don't have a book about that bat," Brownie said. "I read about it in one of the encyclopedias in the library."

"Do you have one?" John asked Bill.

"Yes. It's in the library in the science building. I didn't know you wanted it or I would have got it for you."

[146]

"Reading a few little old books on bats won't take long," Jack said. "Can we play high-over tomorrow night?"

"But I have one more thing to do," John said. "I brought a tennis racket all the way from Chicago and I haven't used it once. I plan to challenge the champion tennis player of College Park to a match."

"She accepts the challenge," was Brownie's happy answer.